Jack's other books include
The Judgment Ring Books:

The Chinook River Princess - June 1, 2000

Staying Away (to be published)

No Tears for an Empty Grave - August 1, 2000

In the Shoes of a Friend (to be published)

Visit http://judgmentring.com

The opinions expressed in Part 1 of this book are those solely of the author and of no one else. The Characters and events in Part 2 of this book are fictitious. Any similarity to real persons, living or dead, is coincidental and not intended.

Published by Expert Systems Programs and Consulting, Inc.

Power to the People
        Electric Power Deregulation
                An Exposé

ISBN 0-9679119-5-8   First Printed Edition

Printed in the United States of America

Power to the People

People

Electric Power Deregulation
An Exposé

Jack Duckworth

Part 1 - Electric Power Deregulation
Everything you Need to Know but Don't Want to Hear

Part 2 ⚊Black Start 2005

Epilogue

Words from the Author

POWER TO THE PEOPLE

Prologue

In our modern world, of ever-increasing progress and complexity, knowledge is power. Those in power have the knowledge and information necessary to allow them to make the decisions that affect the rest of society and to keep themselves in power. If the masses have access to the same information as those in power then they can evaluate the quality of the decision making and the motives of those making the decisions. When I say *those in power* most people will assume I mean our elected government officials. It is usually our elected government officials who are in power—making the laws and rules we live by—but sometimes those with economic power have even more control than our elected representatives..

This book will hopefully give some knowledge and hence *Power to the People.*

POWER TO THE PEOPLE

Part 1

Electric Power Deregulation
Everything you Need to Know
but Don't Want to Hear

Deregulation is forcing the nation into serious shortages of generating and transmission capacity, which will ultimately result in widespread-rotating-local and regional blackouts.

The Business of Electric Power Supply

All of the facilities needed to generate, transmit, and distribute electric power cost money, as does the servicing of all the equipment that needs to be kept operational. On average it costs approximately as much to transmit and distribute electric power as it does to generate it, so that about half of a customer's electric bill pays for generation and the other half pays for transmission and distribution.

On the generation side of the equation some of the costs to generate power are fixed and other costs are variable. For example the costs for building any facilities needed to generate power such as the powerhouses, turbines, generators, fuel storage facilities, fuel delivery equipment, maintenance trucks, etc. are fixed because the payments for money borrowed to build the facilities must be made no matter how much power the generating plants produce or even if they don't produce one kilowatt hour of energy. Other costs of electric power generation are variable because they change depending on how much energy the plants produce. The cost of the fuel and a good portion of the cost of labor to operate and maintain the generation plants are variable. If a generating plant doesn't generate any power, its owner doesn't pay any of the variable costs but still has to pay all of the fixed costs associated with the plant.

The combined electric loads of all customers causes a varying demand for power which is influenced by the life styles of the customers. The lowest electrical loads occur in the spring or fall when mild temperatures are prevalent, and in the wee hours of the morning when everyone, except teenagers, are home in bed. Electrical loads are higher in the winter and summer seasons due to heating and air-conditioning loads. Electrical loads vary throughout the day and from day to day based on the collective pattern of activities of the human population.

The greatest load each year, on an electric power system, occurs on one day, during the normal peak load hours, in either the summer or winter months, depending on how far north the customers are. Most of the lower forty-eight states have summer peaking power systems because over the years more and more buildings and homes have installed air-conditioning. A few northern areas near the Canadian border still have winter peaking systems because of the high demand of electric heating when the temperatures drop into the double-digit negative range. The pattern of rising and falling electric demand throughout the days and the various seasons of the year results in a peak-hour capacity demand sometime in the year and a total energy usage, which on average is only about 53.6 percent of how much energy would be used if the load of the peak-load hour continued every hour for the whole year[1]. This means that, in effect, all of the generating capacity in the country stands idle for 46.4 percent of every year. Of course some of that idle time is put to good use by the generating companies to perform their regular scheduled generating plant maintenance. The greater the amount of time the generating capacity stands idle the higher the cost of the energy has to be in order to cover the fixed costs of the generating plants. The generating companies strive to keep the idle time of their generators at a minimum to keep the cost of their energy down. Generating companies are not eager to install extra or reserve capacity to sit idle until those unusual years when will be needed.

The Regulated Power Market

Under the regulated-monopoly electric power market system in the United States, a utility is assigned a geographic area of responsibility, in which it has exclusive rights to market electric power to end-use

---

[1]   On average, each year electric generators in the United States generate about 53.6 percent of the energy they could generate if they were operated at full load continuously (8,760 hours per year). According to EIA's Electric Power Statistics, U.S. generating companies in 1999 had 785,990 megawatts of generating capability which produced 3,691 billion kilowatt hours of energy.

customers and exclusive responsibility to provide reliable electric service to those customers. This exclusivity is generally referred to as a franchise. Under the franchise philosophy, the utility constructs all of the generation, transmission and distribution facilities necessary to provide reliable electric service to the customers and is allowed to charge electric service rates to its customers to recover its costs plus a reasonable rate of return on the capital it invested in facilities. The utility is allowed to charge its customers, in its electric rates, enough to pay its costs plus a reasonable rate of return to its stockholders.

Before a regulated utility can build any new facilities it must get prior approval from the state regulatory authority, which is generally the public utility commission (PUC) of the state in which the utility operates. The PUC does independent studies to determine if the proposed new facilities are needed and are the least cost facilities to do the intended job. If the PUC determines that the proposed facilities are needed and will do the intended job at the least cost, then the PUC approves the construction and allows the new facilities, when completed, to be included in the utility's rate base.

In the regulated electric power industry, a utility is responsible for the generation and distribution of power to the end-use customers and in the event of failure of the electric power service, it is a simple matter to assign blame and exact justice. A utility must install enough generation, transmission and distribution capacity to meet all of its customers' needs under any foreseeable conditions. The utility must evaluate its customers seasonal usage patterns under various weather conditions and must evaluate its capacity to provide sufficient power under all foreseeable failure conditions. It determines the expected load requirements of all of its customers under normal conditions and then determines what additional capacity (reserve) it must have above that expected demand to meet loads under adverse conditions, assuming worst-case transmission and generation facilities failure.

The capital costs of building the capacity to meet the reserve requirements, which are independently verified by the PUC, are allowed to be included in the utility's rate base so that all of the customers share the cost for the high level of reliability. The added cost of reliability, in the regulated of electric power supply, does not appear to be very much because it is distributed over every kilowatt hour of energy used by the customers. Based on an assumed average generation plant factor of 53.6 percent, the cost of maintaining a 20-percent reserve margin using combined-cycle-combustion-turbine generating plants would be less than one-half cent per kilowatt hour (0.447cents), if spread over all of a utility's electricity sales.

The calculation is performed like so:

> In a highly reliable electric power system, 1,000 kilowatts of customer peak load requires 1,000 kilowatts of generating capacity and 200 kilowatts of reserve capacity (20 Percent of peak load requirements). On average, each 1,000 kilowatts of customer peak load represents an average annual energy use of 4,695,360 kilowatt hours at a load factor of 53.6

percent. The annual cost of 200 kilowatts of reserve capacity from combined-cycle-combustion-turbine generating plants is $21,000 (200 kilowatts times $105 per kilowatt per year). Therefore the cost per kilowatt hour of total energy generation, for a 20-percent reserve margin, is $21,000 divided by 4,695,360 kWh or $0.0044725 per kilowatt hour.

In a regulated electric power system everything is scrutinized, evaluated, checked, approved, and controlled. In addition, reliability of service is assured because the state PUC's require that the utilities maintain adequate generating and transmission reserves.

The drive for deregulation of the electric power industry is based on the assumption that without competition between like suppliers, companies get sloppy, don't provide the lowest cost service possible, and the customer pays higher rates than he would under competition where the sloppy are run out of business.

There are many who question the validity of the assumption that the utilities under our regulated-monopolistic power supply system had grown sloppy. They could grow sloppy only if the various PUC's allowed them to grow sloppy and the consensus is the PUC's were tenacious in their regulation of the industry.

The Deregulated Power Market

In the United States' developing deregulated power market, it is only the generation of electricity that will be truly deregulated. In such a market, virtually anyone with capital resources can build or buy a generating plant and get into the business of selling kilowatt hours of energy. For generating companies (GENCO's) electricity is a commodity like any other and they sell their electric energy either through contracts or through open market bidding.

In the deregulated power market, the transmission/distribution companies (TRANSCO's) will still be monopolies and will have exclusive rights to transmit and distribute the electrical power to the end-use or retail customers in their franchised service area. The problem in trying to describe how the deregulated market will work is the fact that it will be different in each state. Each state is designing its own model for what deregulation should look like. In some states the TRANSCO's will have to buy their energy from the free power generation market and sell it, at its cost including a reasonable rate of return on its investment, to the end-use customers. In other states, the TRANSCO's may only transmit energy at a cost to the energy generation companies who will contract with the end-use customers directly. In such cases, the consumer will have to shop around to find what he believes is the best deal for energy, based on all the honest advertising he sees on TV, hears on the radio, and gets from supper-time calls from telephone solicitors.

If the deregulated market operates as it should, and there is no reason to believe it won't, the cost of electricity in the long term will be less than it would be in a continuing regulated monopolistic market. However, the quality of the electric service may be severely diminished as it has been in the telephone, railroad, and airline industries.

The question of paramount concern to every citizen is, "How will deregulation change my life?" Americans don't want to hear the dogma, "Free markets foster competition and lower prices." They want the straight skinny. The straight skinny on just what the free electric power market is going to mean to the average consumer is not available from any utility, state public utility commission or federal agency. It's not available because the people who pushed for deregulation, embraced it and finally are implementing it, don't know what deregulation is really going to mean to the average electric customer. They have embraced the deregulation philosophy and have run to it with open arms, not knowing for sure if they were running into the arms of a lover or a monster.

The country has scores of years of experience operating a regulated electric power industry and none, nada, zip experience operating a deregulated power industry. When you ask the economic experts how it will work they answer "very well" but if you ask for details they say, "We don't know exactly how something in particular will take place in a deregulated market, but it will be better and cheaper than in a regulated market." It's the old we-don't- know-but-trust-us philosophy of leadership.

The problem with the we-don't-know-but-trust-us philosophy is the fact that the electric power customers are forced to put forth unlimited amount of blind trust but if the experts have failed to foresee some problem it is the customers who will have to foot the bill or suffer the consequences of a major oversight.

Is higher priced electricity the worst consequence of a failure to foresee how deregulation will work? Not really. We could have higher cost electricity at least temporarily but we Americans have always had to suffer the consequences of "brain storms" of leadership. Higher priced electricity is a possibility but only a minor side effect of deregulation.

If a backfire in the price of electricity under deregulation is not the worst possible consequence of deregulation, what is? The answer is simple, straight forward, and predictable — the decline or decay in the reliability of the nation's electrical power supply.

The Natural Decline of Reliability of Service in a Deregulated Market.

To understand how deregulation may undermine reliability of the electric power supply one must understand what makes a reliable electric power system, understand the nature of the free market, understand the motivations of the players in the market, and finally understand how the players will react to the various pressures of the free market.

As I stated earlier, there must be an excess of generating capacity under normal weather and electric generating conditions so that under adverse conditions there will still be enough generating capacity to meet the demand for electricity. In the past it was the regulators who forced the electric utilities to maintain adequate reserves and the cost of maintaining those reserves (about a half-cent per kWh) was passed on to the customers in each kilowatt hour of energy they purchased.

In our currently evolving free power market who is responsible to ensure adequate generation and transmission reserves? Is it the GENCO's who build the generating plants and sell the power to the TRANSCO's or power retailers? No, it is not the GENCO's. The GENCO's build only the generating plants that they believe they can pay for by their sales of electric energy to the TRANSCO's or retailers. Is it the TRANSCO's or power retailers? No, it is not the TRANSCO's or power retailers because they are forbidden to build or own generating plants. They can only purchase energy from GENCO's *if it is available*.

"If the GENCO's aren't responsible to ensure adequate generation capacity and the TRANSCO's and power retailers aren't responsible to ensure adequate generation capacity then who is?"

"It's the market!" The experts say.

"Who in the Market?"

"No one in particular in the market, it's just the free market itself."

"How?"Americans ask, truly perplexed.

"We don't know exactly how, but the free market will ensure adequate capacity."

That's the typical dialogue when anyone broaches the subject with the deregulation experts who are supposed to be leading the deregulation charge. There is an pervasive and overwhelming faith by those who are pushing the deregulation envelope that everything will better under deregulation in a totally free market. They are convinced that a free market for any commodity, with no oversight or checks and balances, will do everything better and cheaper than will a regulated market. However, there are functions which a free market cannot, or will not, perform and those functions must be forced upon the market in the form of requirements or regulations.

How Generating Capacity Reserves
Look to a GENCO

What do generating capacity reserves look like to a generating company? The answer is very simple, they look like an anvil tied around the generating company's neck. If I am a generating company in a free market I must keep the price of the electricity I generate as low as possible—at least as low as my competitor—or no one will buy from me and I'll go out of business. How can I keep the cost of my electricity low? Since I have to pay the interest on the loan I took out to buy my generator whether or not I run my generator at all, the more electricity I can sell the lower the cost will be and the more competitive I will be.

What happens if I build too little generating capacity? Nothing bad, in fact good things happen because likely I'll be able to sell more energy at lower prices than I could if I build more capacity, which would force me to raise my prices.

What happens if I build too much capacity? If I build to much capacity really nasty things happen because too much capacity means I have some capacity sitting idle that almost never generates any energy for sale. I'm not covering my costs well and my prices for the electricity that I do sell has to be higher to cover the cost of my idle equipment. Since I have higher prices I can't compete effectively with my competitors and I might be driven out of business.

The bottom line for the GENCO's is a shortage of capacity can't hurt them, but surplus capacity can increase their costs and literally drive them out of business. How difficult do you think it is to convince a GENCO to build additional generating capacity in a market that has sufficient capacity to meet the expected demands of customers under normal conditions (zero reserve margin)? How difficult do you think it is to convince a GENCO to build more generating capacity, which it won't likely be able to sell unless the weather gets really nasty or some unforeseen calamity strikes and knocks a bunch of generators off line? Let's just say it's difficult to convince any GENCO to stick it's corporate neck out and build additional generating capacity that may just destroy its competitive position in the free electric power market.

Let's take a realistic look at what it takes and what it costs to make a reliable electric power system before we jump into the free power market assuming that it will accomplish everything that the regulators forced the utilities to do in the regulated monopolistic market. In a power system with adequate reserves (conservatively 20 percent reserve margin over peak load requirements), how long is it between times when all of the combined reserve capacity in a region is called upon to actually generate energy to meet loads? It can be anywhere from a few years or decades to forever.

In a system with adequate reserves some reserve generating capacity will sit for several years without being needed, some reserve generating capacity will sit idle for one or several decades, and some capacity will sit forever without having to generate a single kilowatt hour of energy. So how much would it cost if we just charged the customer for the energy generated by that reserve capacity when the customer actually uses it? The number is so high it's off the charts. Just as an example, lets assume that I am a GENCO and an energy retailer comes to me to buy some reserve capacity. If he comes and says he'll pay for me to install some reserve capacity that he will need during critical weather conditions I will ask him how he intends to pay for the reserve capacity. If he says he will pay a flat fee every month of every year whether or not he ever calls upon it, I will charge him $8.75 every month for each kilowatt of capacity that I have to build and keep in reserve. If on the other hand he says, "I'll pay you for every kilowatt hour of energy that I need during adverse weather conditions," I have a serious problem. The serious problem is that I have no idea exactly how much energy he will need or when he will need it. If he needs to buy all of the energy generated from one kilowatt of capacity for eight hours every weekday for one week every month (2,080 kWh per year), I will need to charge him 5 cents per kilowatt hour of energy to cover my cost of the reserve capacity which is $105 per kilowatt of capacity per year. If on the other hand, he needs to buy all the energy from one kilowatt of capacity for an eight-hour peak load which will occur only on the hottest summer day that will occur, on average, once every ten years, (8 kWh in ten years) I will need to charge him $131.25 for each kilowatt hour of energy I sell him to cover my cost of the reserve capacity which is $1,050 ($105 per kilowatt per year for ten years). That's a cost 1,875 times as great as the average cost of electricity in the retail market. You say, "that's ridiculous because in the regulated market we never paid that much for reserves." I say you're wrong, people paid the same amounts for reserve capacity in the regulated market but it wasn't an issue because people paid a little bit for that expensive reserve capacity in every kilowatt hour of energy they bought. They paid the same amount overall, it's just that the price for individual blocks of energy never got that high.

In a regulated market the same costs were paid but were never evident. Now in a free market the true cost of reserve capacity, that is rarely if ever used, shows up on an invoice when it's actually needed and the public goes nuts when it gets the bill.

It's just that we're not used to paying for generating capacity reserves only when we use them; we're used to paying for reserves like we pay for life insurance, all the time at a fixed rate.

In a regulated power market the regulators can force the utilities to build adequate reserve capacity that it deems necessary and in the public's best interest, because the cost is automatically passed on to the power consumers in the approved electric rates. However, in a free market, in which there are no mandated reserve requirements, GENCO's will only build adequate reserve capacity if they're sure they can sell it at profitable rates.

Stressing the Electric System

How have the new GENCO's been behaving in the electric power market as it has slowly gravitated away from regulation and toward a free market? They have been reacting perfectly predictably, doing their level best to cut costs and trim any unnecessary expenses. Every GENCO has been cutting preventative maintenance costs, trimming its payroll and, above all, avoiding any new capital expenditures, especially the capital expenditures associated with building new generating capacity. If the GENCO's have been avoiding building new generating capacity then the data should show it, shouldn't it? Yes it should and the data does show it.

In its 1978 publication "Hydroelectric Power Evaluation" the Federal Energy Regulatory Commission stated that the utilities maintain reserve capacities ranging from fifteen percent to twenty-five percent of peak load requirements. That means the lowest reserve capacity for any utility in the country at that time was fifteen percent. If one studies the loads and resource data published by the North American Electric Reliability Council (NERC) one will see that reserve margins have been decaying steadily ever since the serious talk of deregulation started. The reserve margins range across the country from a low of 10 percent in California to a high of twenty six percent in Oklahoma with a national average of about 16.1 percent (see Table 1 page 34).

In years past, (the good ole days) reserves were calculated based on total generating capacity owned by the utilities and firm purchases of capacity under contract by the utilities. Now it appears from their data that NERC includes capacity that would have to be purchased (not necessarily under firm contract) from others in order to meet the stated reserve capacity objectives. If one studies the data for all of the ten reporting reliability council regions in the lower 48, one will see that the combined total of summertime net purchases exceeds combined net sales by about 33,000 megawatts of capacity (see Table 2 page 19). That means that in the summer of 2001 the whole lower 48 states would have had to purchase about 33,000 megawatts of capacity to meet their stated reserve requirements and purchase it from Canada. It is evident that over the past decade the U.S. utilities, in preparation for deregulation, have been slowing their construction of new capacity and increasing their planned purchases of reserve capacity from Canada, which makes perfect economic sense in a fully deregulated power market. What is the downside of letting this policy continue? The downside is that ultimately even Canada with it's winter peaking system will run out of surplus summer capacity and its sales will not be able prevent serious reliability problems for us. The downside is also that serious problems develop in the transmission system when it's called upon to transmit large amounts of power from Canada to the eastern mid-west and the southeastern seaboard, which it was never designed to do.

The more the GENCO's avoid building their own capacity near their customers and continue to purchase distant power, the more stress they put on the country's transmission system.. When the transmission system, or backbone of the country fails, the national security is threatened because the country will suffer widespread power failures.

Following is a scenario which could have happened in the summer in 2001 but luckily didn't:

The Southeastern Electric Reliability Council (SERC), which includes, at least, parts of the states of Florida, Alabama, Georgia, Mississippi, Tennessee, Kentucky, North Carolina, South Carolina, and Virginia, has the lowest owned reserve capacity margin in the whole country and planned on purchasing up to 18,900 megawatts of capacity to meet extreme summer load conditions if they were to occur in 2001 (Table 2 page 35). Just north of the SERC council region is the ECAR region, which includes, at least, parts of the states of Kentucky, Virginia, West Virginia, Maryland, Pennsylvania, Ohio, Indiana, and Michigan. It intended to purchase 6,100 megawatts of capacity also in the summer of 2001 to meets its reserve needs. Since the whole combination of reliability councils in the lower 48 states are net purchasers of summer reserve capacity, the 25,000 megawatts of purchased capacity for SERC and ECAR would ultimately come from Canada through a myriad of transmission lines across all of the states, which lie between Canada and the ECAR and SERC power customers. The whole US had planned to purchase 33,000 megawatts of reserve capacity from Canada and it should raise a red flag when seventy-five percent of the total outside purchases would go to twenty-percent of the area in the U.S.

In its summer 2001 assessment, NERC stated that the New England Electric Reliability council could be in trouble in the summer of 2001. Although the region showed having 4,000 megawatts of reserve capacity, most of it was in Quebec and due to transmission limitations only 1,000 megawatts of capacity could be assured. If the New England states couldn't expect to get much reserve capacity relief from Quebec because of transmission constraints then what would happen when SERC, which is hundreds of miles further away, tried to suck 18,900 megawatts of capacity through the transmission system and ECAR adjacent to and directly north of SERC tried to suck 6,100 megawatts of capacity through most of the same transmission circuits? If the eastern mid-west part of the country had suffered an extreme heat wave in the summer of 2001, SERC and ECAR would have tried to pull power down from the north and would likely have overloaded the transmission system. The most overloaded lines would have overheated and have had to be taken out of service to prevent failure. That loss of transmission capacity would have forced increased loads on the remaining transmission lines which would have, in turn, been overloaded and have had to removed from service. Transmission failures in the eastern mid-west would then have caused a strain on the adjacent reliability areas in the mid-west and on the east coast. If the heat wave would have been wide spread and the eastern and mid-western councils didn't quickly cut the transmission ties to SERC and ECAR, to contain the power outage, the whole eastern half of the country could have been pulled into a massive power failure that could have taken as much as to three or four days to recover from.

It was pure luck (a lot of good luck) the above scenario did not come to pass in the summer of 2001. Iif action is not taken soon to stem the tide of decaying reserve margins, the failure scenario I described above will come to pass in the summer of 2002, 2003, 2004, 2005 or whenever a severe summer heat wave meets an unforseen severe generating capacity or transmission failure.

I find it interesting that in its 2001 Summer Reliability Assessment NERC stated with respect to the ECAR council area:

> It is anticipated that the transmission system could be constrained as a result of generation unit unavailability and/or economic transactions that have historically resulted in large unanticipated power flows within in and through the region.

In the context of the statement, it's clear that the word *constrained* should have been more appropriately *overloaded*. It's also clear that situations of *unit unavailability and or economic transactions* referred to unscheduled generating plant outages and the importation of power from outside the region because of insufficiency of owned reserves within the region to meet the outage conditions. How can anyone consider as *unanticipated*, large power flows needed to import reserves from outside the region to meet power plant outages, which are expected (by definition) to be covered by reserves?

NERC's 2001 summer Reliability Assessment also stated:

> During summer 2000, heavy north-to-south transactions from and through the western ECAR network resulted in heavy

> transmission loading in the southwestern
> portion of the ECAR system.

Again it's interesting that NERC only mentioned the fact that heavy north-south transactions caused heavy transmission loading in the region without concluding the cause of the heavy transmission loading was excessive purchases of reserves from outside the combined ECAR-SERC region from the north.

With respect to the SERC region, the 2001 summer reliability assessment stated in part:

> Heavy north-to-south transfers over the
> last two summers have caused some
> voltage depression and severely stressed
> the SERC transmission systems.

This is a read-between-the-lines conclusion that the SERC's transmission systems are being overloaded, as should be expected due to SERC's over-subscription to outside purchases of reserve capacity. It's obvious from the data that the generating companies in the ECAR and SERC regions are not constructing the generation resources the regions need to meet reserve requirements. To keep their bottom lines a low as possible, the generating companies are depending on outside resources to the extent that the situation is quickly becoming so severe as to threaten the stability of the neighboring council areas as well as their own.

On the introduction page of NERC's website at http://www.nerc.com, NERC stated, as of July 15, 2001:

In response to industry changes, NERC is in the process of transforming itself into NAERO -- the North American Electric Reliability Organization. NAERO's mission will be to develop, promote, and enforce standards for a reliable North American bulk electric system. Under the existing system, compliance is mandatory but it is not enforceable. NERC is working with its members to incorporate enforcement through the development of contracts between the Regions and their members. NERC is seeking federal legislation in the U.S. to ensure that NERC and its Regions have the statutory authority to enforce compliance with reliability standards among all market participants.

Until such time as NERC acquires some enforcement authority and independence from the power companies, it will be relegated to making non-threatening assessments of the national electric power system such as those above. NERC's assessments imply serious reliability problems but don't point fingers where they need to be pointed and don't propose solutions which would require some regulatory enforcement clout.

The Risks of Uncertainty Faced by the Generation Companies

The free power market is so volatile that no one can predict with any degree of accuracy what's going to happen to capacity reserve margins even one year down the road. NERC's 2000-2009 Electric Supply and Demand Estimates showed that New England was expected to have a summer 2001 reserve capacity margin of about 25.5 percent. NERC's 2001 Summer Assessment, which came out in May 2001, showed that New England was expected to have a summer 2001 reserve capacity margin of about 12.6 percent. The fact that the power supply experts cannot predict what generating capacity reserves will be twelve months in advance, with better than 50-percent accuracy, is downright scary, or at least should be to anyone who cares if the nation's lights stay on or go out. The difference between the reserve capacity estimates only 12 months apart represents the difference between a power supply region being fat with capacity reserves and so short on reserves that power supply curtailments are likely. We're in deep trouble if we let the unregulated free market be the determinate for how much reserve capacity is actually constructed, when, in a free market, it cannot be determined if there will be excess capacity reserve or extreme reserve capacity shortage twelve month in advance. We're in deep trouble because it takes a minimum of two years and an average of 4 years to bring new generating capacity on line. Under these kinds of conditions, no one can be sure that two years from today the entire electric power system of the country won't be in danger of shutting down from a cascading power failure.

Lessons of the California Experience

California is known for always being on the cutting edge in every field of endeavor. It's now first and breaking new ground in its failure to maintain adequate reserve margins. California is showing the rest of the country what it means to be short on generating capacity. Although Californians did it to themselves out of a desire to create a better and cleaner world, the lesson is none the less valuable because what California did voluntarily to itself, the GENCO's are now doing to the rest of the country out of economic necessity.

California had been working for years to cut its construction of new generating facilities within its borders and to make due by reducing load requirements through conservation. California has been resisting the evils (developing their resources) of a growing economy for more than twenty years and has achieved landmark levels of electric power conservation. In getting where they are, they have strained all outside power markets to the limit in the effort to avoid building new capacity in-state. I can remember about twenty years ago one of the large California utilities tried to get approval to construct a mine-mouth, coal-fueled electric generating plant in Wyoming because California wouldn't approve of such a plant within its borders. The governor of Wyoming told the utility that it could not construct the plant in Wyoming. He said that if the Californians wanted power from economical coal they could build the plant in California and Wyoming would ship the coal to them, so they could burn it in their own state. Since that time, California had been scouring the western power markets for any unclaimed electric generation. They are buying every bit of power that isn't needed by the other power systems to meet their own load requirements. By such efforts California has avoided building new capacity to the limits of theoretical possibility. With the advent of deregulation and the generation companies' reluctance to build new capacity anywhere, California has now hit the capacity wall. Californians now claim that everyone is conspiring against them by refusing to sell them the capacity they need at prices they like but, in reality, the whole western market has sold them everything they can possibly sell them and it's still not enough to keep the Californians' heads above water.

California is claiming that the generating companies are charging exorbitant prices for their power during peak load times which are many times greater than the generating companies' costs. However in a free market, in which the cost of reserve capacity, as well as operating capacity, is included in the cost of purchasing energy, it's impossible to determine a generation company's cost of energy generation before the end of any fiscal year. California had set up rules for its free market which forbade the power purchasers from buying any power on a long-term contract. It required that all power purchasers buy their power on the spot market, where in times of surplus prices drop to the floor or even into the basement and in times of shortage prices go through the roof and even into the stratosphere.

In a spot market, the generation companies have no idea what their costs of generation are. Although they know what the variable costs of the generation will be for each kilowatt hour of energy generated, they don't know what their fixed charges for each kilowatt hour of energy will be because the don't know until the end of their fiscal year how much energy they will have sold. When the power generating companies don't know how much energy they will ultimately sell they are forced to charge whatever the market will bear in times of shortage to make sure they make enough revenue to cover their annual fixed costs.   Most regions of the country are now following California down that same road toward generating capacity shortages. In a perverse way, the Californians are doing us a service by showing us what the road is going to look like. It does not matter whether, like in California, the regulators chose to not approve construction of the needed reserve capacity, driven by a desire to breathe clean air or, rather, generation companies in a free market choose to not build needed reserve capacity because its not in their best economic interest. Either way, the results are the same, inadequate reserve capacity margins, system voltage reductions, load shedding, and rotating blackouts. As it has always been in the past, California leads the way—as goes California, ultimately, so goes the rest of the country.

The major shortcoming of the whole deregulation process is the fact that those making the decisions on what deregulation should look like are economists and lawyers, who have a very shallow understanding of the physics of electricity and of the nuts and bolts of power generation, transmission, distribution and sale. They are steeped in theory and short on real experience—heavy on book learning and light on electric system power operations experience. The little bit they know about the real physics of the power supply is being spoon fed to them by the new power generating entrepreneurs, who have their own agendas and profit margins to protect.

The free market economists and lawyers see no differences between the markets for Beeny Babies and electric power. They think that supply, demand, and price will always work interactively to maintain an equitable balance without any outside interaction or control. If there is a run on Beeny Babies in New York City then the price will go up for a short time and the suppliers will ship more Beeny Babies to the city to make more sales and the price will come back in line. They apply the same line of reasoning to the electric power market and come to the conclusion that any shortage in power will cause a temporary increase in price, but that power suppliers will build whatever new plants are needed and will ship in power to make more money and the price will come back down. The differences in the markets are the time it takes to make Beeny Babies versus the time it takes to build generating plants; and the unlimited capacity of the trucking industry to carry as many Beeny Babies as anyone could possibly need to anywhere in the country, versus the limited national electric transmission capacity.

The deregulation purists believe that since there is a four-hour time difference between California and New York, and the electrical peak loads occur four hours apart, if California needs power it can flow from New York over all the transmission lines across the country to California and, conversely, if New York needs power it can flow from California. These people don't understand the physical limitations of the transmission of electrical power. They honestly believe that the electric power system of this country is like a lake; when anyone takes a bucket of water from anywhere in the lake the water from all over the lake moves the fill the hole left by the missing bucket of water and whenever anyone takes a kilowatt hour of energy from the electric power system anywhere in the country power moves from all over the country to fill hole left by the missing kilowatt hour of energy .

It's too bad that kilowatt hours aren't Beeny Babies and electric power systems aren't lakes because, if they were, deregulation would be a smooth road indeed. Kilowatt hours aren't Beeny Babies and electric power systems aren't lakes—that's a fact we're going to have to live with. The path to electric power deregulation is no super highway; it's a narrow, winding, rough, gravel, country lane; it's full of chuck holes and the drivers of the deregulation bus can't be hamstrung or blindfolded.

The previous administration let let lawyers and economists shape the country's electric deregulation policy for the eight years it was in power and currently the country's deregulation policy is in sad shape. Hopefully the new administration will bring in some engineers who really understand the issues, take the blindfolded economists and lawyers out of the driver's seat, and give NERC some independence and enforcement teeth. In short, we can only hope that the new administration in Washington will get the electric deregulation bus off the back roads of America and back on the interstate highways.

The Telephone and Airline Deregulation Examples

Whenever the proponents of power deregulation need examples to convince the skeptics that deregulation works, they march out their deregulated telephone and airline industries as examples of how deregulation works to get costs of service down.

There are those who may question the true economic savings when they realize that before deregulation of the telephone industry Ma Bell was going to have fiber optic telephone service to every home in America before 1980 and now, in the new millennium, local phone facilities are so poor and over-loaded in many areas of the country (including many suburbs of Washington D.C.) that high-speed DSL INTERNET service is physically impossible to install . Others may question the true economic savings when they try to get an airline flight to Monroe, Louisiana on a holiday or are given an individual serving cereal box for breakfast on the $1,200 round-trip flight.

Let's not dwell on all of the economic savings that we get from the deregulated telephone and airline industries but rather evaluate the reliability of their service, which is the primary problem now facing the deregulated power industry. The airline and telephone industries happen to be perfect examples to illustrate what lies ahead for the electric power industry and why reserve capacity deficits should be no surprise to those pushing for deregulation.

Before deregulation of the telephone industry any citizen could pick up his or her telephone on any day of any year and call his or her mother, or whomever, and have the call go through. Following deregulation it has become accepted that when one calls a loved one on Mother's Day, Thanksgiving, Christmas, Valentine's day or any other highly observed holiday one likely will hear, "We're sorry, but all circuits are busy. Please try your call again later."

Before deregulation of the airline industry any citizen could reserve a seat on a flight to anywhere in the country on any day close to the highly observed holidays. Following deregulation of the airlines it has become expected that one will show up at the gate for a flight on which he or she has a reserved seat only to find that six other people are expecting to sit in the same seat with him or her. Before deregulation you would never hear an airline attendant stand at the front of the isle in the airplane and say, "We will give a free voucher for a ticket to anyone to anywhere this airline flies on any day that is not close to any holiday, if you give up your seat to another passenger who also has a reserved seat on this flight." Of course it should be noted that it wasn't the airlines' idea to bribe boarded customers to give up their seats for others. The airlines attitude in the early days of free competition was that while they were sorry that some passengers with confirmed reservations had to be turned away at the gate, they were not responsible to ensure that everyone had a seat in a free market. It was the Federal Aviation Administration and the threat of a congressional bill that forced the airlines to honor confirmed reservations by buying back airline seats. So even in the free market of airline transportation, regulators and lawmakers have to step in, every once in a while, to ensure the system works efficiently.

What happened to the telephone and airline industries is exactly what one should expect when an industry is deregulated. In a newly deregulated market every supplier cuts reserve margins to the bone in order to reduce its costs so it can be more competitive. It's a fact that when any industry providing a service or product is deregulated, it will reduce inventory or reserves to be more competitive. The question is, "Can we as a nation afford to have electric power reserves cut like the airlines cut the reserve supply of its seats or the telephone companies cut the reserve supply of their telephone circuits?" The answer is an unequivocal "No!"

With telephone service it may be annoying to hear the "all circuits are busy" recording but what's the downside of not being able to call your mother at 8 pm on Mother's Day? Okay she'll think you don't love her anymore but that makes you even because you thought she didn't love you when you were six and you ran away from home to spite her.

With airline service, it may be annoying to have to wait ten extra minutes for an airline attendant to bribe another passenger to come off the plane to make room for you because they don't have the capacity they need for peak load days, but what's the downside of that? You get annoyed and the plane is a few minutes more late than the deregulated airlines' planes are regularly late but it's really no big deal.

In the electric power industry, the inadequate-reserve-capacity equivalents of the all-circuits-are-busy telephone recording and the bribe-a-passenger-for-a-seat airline flight delay are voltage reductions, rotating blackouts and total regional electric system failures.

While the proponents of deregulation may hold up the telephone and airline industries as examples of how deregulation is supposed to work, I hope they will someday grasp the reality that inadequate electric power reserves are not in any way equivalent to, or as acceptable as, inadequate telephone circuit reserves and inadequate airline seat reserves.

It would be nice if during a power capacity deficit situation one could turn on a light switch and have a recorded message come on saying something like: "We are sorry but all available generating capacity is already running at full load. If you want to turn on this light you must first turn off another light of equal or greater wattage, or go downstairs and unplug your freezer," but the electric power system is not set up to operate that way. The fact is when too many people use too much power, the system voltage drops and if the TRANSCO's or power retailers don't throw enough big switches, cutting off large blocks of customers from electric power, the whole system will be subjected to a cascading collapse and ultimately the *Big Dark* will extend from shore to shining shore.

The electric power system of this country is too important and essential to the safety and welfare of all of its citizens, and to the national security, to be left totally to the vagaries of the free market. To say that we will have adequate electrical generating reserve margins if the market works as it's *supposed to* is equivalent to playing Russian roulette with a gun the temple of the entire nation. Oh, Lord save us from the free-market purists who would risk it all to keep all markets free from any encumbrances, rules, or controls. Free markets need to be like free speech–free only to the extent that they don't do harm to our citizens or to the national security.

How to Fall Short of Adequate
Generating Capacity Reserves

When a free market takes a detour in the wrong direction or behaves in an unexpected and unacceptable manner then those in a position of authority have the obligation to step in with rules or procedures to correct the unacceptable behavior. I can think of no free market that is totally free and which can operate without any intervention. The telephone industry is supposed to be an unregulated market, but I keep hearing about what businesses telephone companies can and can't participate in and which cable companies can or cannot offer telephone service, so it's clear that the telephone industry is free only to the extent that it does not operate to the detriment of the public interest. In a similar way the airline industry is deregulated but it still must meet certain safety and maintenance standards set by the Federal Aviation Administration. Even the free economic system of the whole United States cannot operate at maximum efficiency without intervention by the Federal Government. We have a free economy but the Federal Reserve is constantly applying corrections to the national economy by raising or lowering the Federal interest rates to either stimulate sales or to curb inflation. Our banking industry is supposed to be a free market also, but the federal government has requirements for how much money each bank must keep in reserve. Why would anyone think that the power industry can operate with less oversight than the other free market industries? Why would anyone believe that the electric power supply for the entire nation can be left to the pressures of a totally free and unfettered market without getting knocked off track in some unwanted and unsafe direction?

It is obvious from all the data available that, if left to its own devices, the deregulated electric power market will allow generating capacity reserve margins to decay to levels which will turn the whole country into a California-look-alike. It will do it not out of a disregard for the national well being but out of economic necessity. In the evolving deregulated power market, just like in nature, only the most fit will survive. No one generating company can afford to be a good citizen and maintain adequate capacity reserve margins so long as any others do not. The reward for being a good citizen in a free market is extinction. The company who maintains adequate reserves will have higher costs than its bad-citizen competitors and will be driven out of the market in bankruptcy. If one looks closely at those who are fighting the hardest to keep the federal government from setting any reliability standards I'm fairly sure one will discover that they are the generating companies currently with the lowest owned reserves of capacity and the highest profit margins.

According to NERC's 2001 summer assessment the various U.S. reliability councils were projected to have the capacity reserve margins shown in Table 1 below.

With capacity margins such as these, the whole country should be in fine shape, but obviously with California hanging on by its fingernails and New England

Table 1. Total Capacity Reserve Margin by NERC Reliability Council

Council	Total Reserve Margin
WSCC	18.4 %
MAPP	21.8 %
SPP	13.5 %
ERCOT	16.8 %
MAIN	15.5 %
ECAR	14.2 %
SERC	13.8 %
FRCC	17.3 %
MAAC	15.1 %
NPCC	17.2 %
Overall	16.1 %

and New York not far behind, something highly significant is not being reflected by the total reserve numbers. The something that's not reflected by the reserve numbers is just how much of those total reserves are owned within the reliability regions and how much is having to come from outside (ultimately from Canada).

According to NERC's 2000-2009 Resource and Loads data, overall, the owned reserves in the reliability councils were projected in 2000 for the summer of 2001 as follows:

Table 2. Total Summer 2001 Owned Capacity Reserve Margin and Capacity Purchases and Sales by NERC Reliability Council

Council	Owned Reserve Margin	Net Purchases or (Sales) in Megawatts
WSCC	19.0 %	(974)
MAPP	-1.0 %	9,141
SPP	9.8 %	1,652
ERCOT	23.6 %	(4,363)
MAIN	12.6 %	1,779
ECAR	8.9 %	6,094
SERC	3.0 %	18,925
FRCC	7.6 %	4,183
MAAC	15.5 %	(241)
NPCC	19.0 %	(2,922)
Overall	11.5 %	33,274

In a free power market, the only way to ensure adequate capacity reserves is to mandate reserves for everyone so no one has an unfair competitive advantage over another. It's not reasonable to expect that the states can mandate adequate reserves, because the GENCO's and TRANSCO's operate across state lines. If the states or even entire regions of the country were to attempt to mandate reserve margins, there would be differences between how the various states or regions employ the mandates and inequities would develop between competitors. In the end, chaos would rein because the market would not provide a level playing field for all the competitors. The only effective means to ensure adequate generating capacity reserves is to mandate them at the federal level for the entire country and ensure that the burden is evenly distributed among and between all of the GENCO's.

ISO New England tried to encourage such reserve margins by making the power purchasers pay fines if they did not purchase adequate reserves. Their thinking was that if they made the TRANSCO's or power retailers pay a fine equal to the cost of the amount of reserve capacity they were short then they would pay that amount in the market for the reserve capacity and the GENCO's would respond by building the needed capacity. They were trying to encourage GENCO's to build plants by using economic carrot-and-stick incentives against the GENCOs' customers and hoping the incentives would be passed on to the GENCO's. In theory the method may work but in practice the ISO's proposed fines were too small in comparison to the risk the GENCO's would have to take.

New England changed it's capacity reserve incentive program twice in as many years. Knowing it takes from two to five years to build a new generating plant, what GENCO is going to commit millions of dollars to an investment that may be economical one day but uneconomical by the time it would be constructed because the market overseer would likely change the rules in midstream.

Another problem with ISO New England's methodology was the penalty they intended to place on the power retailers for not having adequate capacity was substantially less than the true market cost of constructing the needed capacity. In that case, which I will demonstrate a bit later, the ISO would fine the power purchasers, at most, $26.25 each year for each kilowatt of reserve capacity they would be short but it would cost the GENCO's $105 each year to provide the capacity for the power purchasers to purchase. In other words, the ISO intended to encourage the GENCO's to construct new $105-per-year capacity on the promise that they would have customers who would purchase the capacity for $26.25 per year. This is the equivalent of the government promising GM or Chrysler that it would provide an unlimited number of customers who would be willing to buy new Chevies or Chryslers for $5,000 each if the two car companies would increase production of the $20,000 cars to meet the increased demand.

The ISO believed that its $8.75-per-kilowatt-month price was the market price for the needed capacity. If one looks at each month by itself, the price seems right. The annual carrying costs, including interest, principal, insurance, fixed operation and maintenance expense and taxes for newly constructed new natural-gas fueled combined-cycle-cycle combustion turbine generating units in today's market is $105 per kilowatt of capacity. If that figure is divided by twelve months, the monthly cost is $8.75 per kilowatt. The problem is the ISO proposed to charge the retailers $8.75 for every kilowatt they were short for the period over which they were short. For New England power retailers, the summer peak season is about three months so that if they failed to have adequate reserves every day for the entire the summer season they would be charged $26.25 ($8.75 times three) for each kilowatt of shortage over the three-month summer season. Therefore the retailers would have to pay a fine of $26.25 or buy enough capacity to meet their reserve requirements. Guess what, no one can buy one kilowatt of summer reserve capacity for $26.25 unless they are buying it from Canada, which is a winter peaking region with excess summer capacity. When a generating company builds a new plant it must pay for the plant all year, that's twelve months at $8.75 per month. No GENCO in the lower 48 states is going to build a new generating plant on the promise that some power retailer will pay for it for three months each year. In the New England market, which is a summer peaking area, everyone has their peak loads in the summer and the loads the rest of the year are lower. If a GENCO were to build a plant to sell power only during the summer months to a power retailer, as the ISO New England envisioned, the GENCO would have eat the remaining $78.75 cost of the capacity because there is no market for the reserve capacity except during the peak-load summer months. In a free market, GENCO's who charge only $26.25 for capacity that costs them $105 will quickly find themselves, like PG&E of California, in Chapter 11 bankruptcy. The bottom line is ISO New England's proposed $8.75 per kilowatt of shortage penalty for power purchasers, who purchase insufficient reserve capacity, would result in zero new construction.

Market penalties and incentives will not cause significant increases in capacity reserves or even cause a slowing in the ongoing decay in the capacity reserves. The GENCO's don't believe the newly developing market will pay the true cost of building new capacity and aren't confident that even if the market promises today to pay the true cost for building new capacity it won't go back on its promise and drop the prices tomorrow. Only direct federal mandates for reserve capacity margins will prevent serious nation-wide reserve capacity shortages in the long term. Because of the long lead time for new power plant construction, even federally mandated reserve capacity margins will not work quickly enough to eliminate the possibility of serious capacity deficits outside of California within the next five years.

Do Price Controls Work?

There are many unknowns in the emerging free power market, but the effectiveness of price controls is not one of them. Price controls totally undermine a free market. Price controls artificially limit the maximum price of a product when the supply becomes short. While in the short run lower maximum prices please the public, in the long term they totally undermine the supply of the product because they discourage investment in new production facilities. They send the message that the consumer is willing to support only the cost of the current levels of production and suppliers cannot afford to construct production facilities that the customers refuse to pay for.

Price controls are a Band-Aid approach to keep the customers from being bled to death by high power costs in shortage situations, but such controls keep the wound (capacity shortages) from healing and ultimately the wound will become infected, the patient will develop blood poisoning and will die. Ways must be found to increase the supplies without letting the consumers avoid the cost of increasing supplies to the detriment of the suppliers. Price controls tell the generating companies that the government does not intend to let them pass on the cost of installing additional reserve capacity to the customers. In response, the generating companies will dig in their heels and refuse to construct additional facilities that may undermine their profitability or their ability to compete in the market.

The Switch from Regional to National Power Markets

The major change in the deregulated power industry is the total switch in the philosophy of power supply. In a regulated power industry the generation and transmission resources are planned and constructed based on a regional need philosophy in which the resources are planned and constructed in a timely fashion to meet projected needs which are determined by detailed studies of consumers use habits, weather conditions, projected changes in demographics, etc. In a deregulated power industry the generation and transmission resources are not planned or constructed based on any projections. Rather, they are constructed in response to a shortage, and the shortage may occur anywhere in the nation because there are no regional boundaries in the deregulated market.

Our current electric power infrastructure developed under a regional-needs-projection philosophy and that is the only experience our power engineers and planners have to draw upon. That is why when asked how the new deregulated power market will operate, they throw up their hands and say, "We don't know how it will work exactly, but we're sure it will work."

The regulated market had an exceptional record of projecting regional electric loads and planning the generating and transmission capacity within the regions to meet those projected needs. The power companies had to depend heavily on their projection expertise because of the long time periods involved in the planning, siting, permitting, and construction of the generating plants and transmission lines. When it takes four to eight years from projection of a generating capacity need to completion of construction of a power plant, and when it takes six to ten years from the projection of a transmission shortfall to completion of construction of a long transmission within one state, accurate projection of future needs is essential if one does not accept failure as an acceptable option.

In the deregulated market, there are no requirements for projections because the philosophy of forecasting, planning and constructing is replaced by the simple philosophy of constructing when a shortage forces a spike in prices. The deregulated power market is purely a reactionary market in which shortages result in price spikes, which inspire entrepreneurs to build resources to make profits. In a deregulated power market the capacity and transmission resource construction will always fall behind because that is the nature of a free market. In a free market there is always either just enough, or not quite enough resource to meet demand. This is the case because no one, planning to make a profit, will build a resource even one day before it is actually needed.

Since generating capacity planning and construction requires an average of six years and transmission capacity planning and construction requires an average of eight years, it is reasonable to assume that generating and transmission capacity will always be about six and eight years, respectively, behind actual needs. Under such a philosophy, temporary shortages under times of extreme conditions are assured. Since moderately-extreme conditions such as wide-spread abnormally high summer temperatures occur on average about every five years, we should expect wide-spread power shortages and blackouts about every five years. Following each such shortage condition, which will be accompanied by price spikes, there will be a rush to plan and construct new capacity to meet the shortage (following the California example). Since it takes so long to plan and construct the new resources, it's reasonable to expect that by the time the new resources are available, they will be inadequate to meet the needs which have continued to grow while the new resources were being planned and constructed. Under power deregulation there will be at least one serious generation shortage somewhere in the nation on average every five years.

The shortfall in resources will be likely be worse than I project above, because construction of needed transmission capacity will be even a more difficult task under deregulation than it was under regulation. The switch from a regional power supply philosophy to a national one will be especially burdensome on the transmission system. Failure to plan resources on a regional-need basis will force significantly more and greater inter-regional transfers of power. The longer the transmission line the longer the time for approval and construction. While it is difficult to acquire the necessary property rights, to do the necessary environmental studies, and to secure the necessary federal, state, and local permits to construct a transmission line within one state, it is much more difficult and time consuming to do the same when crossing numerous states. So that not only will the identification of need for additional transmission capacity be delayed under deregulation, but the time needed for the construction of extra-long, inter-regional transmission lines will increase. Delays in resource construction unavoidably increase the frequency and magnitude of shortages.

The Need for Federally-Mandated Reserve Requirements

The federal government needs to get seriously involved in mandating adequate generating capacity reserves near the load centers (not many hundreds of miles distant) in order to ensure the well being of all its citizens and the national security. One way that the Federal Government could mandate adequate reserves, that would keep the playing field level for all of the competing GENCO's, is to mandate a percentage reserve margin for all GENCO's. For example all of the GENCO's could be required to maintain reserve margins of some fixed number, such as 20 percent. Under such a requirement the GENCO's could only market up to 80 percent of their owned capacity under normal peak load conditions and could market the remaining 20 percent of their owned capacity in some kind of incremental steps only under specified increasingly dire load conditions, such as the many incremental corrective action steps defined in New England Power Pool's Operating Procedure Number 4 for capacity deficit situations. There are any number of ways to package a capacity reserve mandate that would apply to all GENCO's proportionately according to their resources, keep the power-market playing field level for all the competitors, and compel the construction of the needed capacity reserves.

The result of such mandated reserve requirements would be an adequate supply of capacity even during times of extreme weather conditions or unusually high generating resource failures. Mandated reserve requirements would guarantee that there wouldn't be extreme shortages which would drive prices to stratospheric levels. As soon as available capacity under the 80-percent market rule would become exhausted, additional capacity would become available under shortage rules and the available capacity would keep prices from rising uncontrollably, as they did in the California market when the available marketable capacity was exhausted. In other words, mandated capacity reserves would reduce the need for load curtailment and would serve to dampen extreme prices without having to implement price caps, which are counter-productive in free markets. The GENCO's would include their costs for reserve capacity in their market energy prices and the costs would be spread over the full spectrum of energy sales rather than concentrated into the very limited energy sales that occur during extreme shortage situations.

The longer the government delays mandating reserve requirements for generating companies, the more severe the impending capacity shortage will become. Even if the government were to establish reserve requirements today it would be several years before any additional new capacity could be available, beyond that which would occur without mandates..

Market Power

Market Power is the term in free-market jargon that refers to the power that some large competitors have to upset the normal interaction of supply and demand to establish prices for a product in order to give themselves an unfair competitive advantage. For example one supplier of a product or service might have such a high percentage of the total sales for the product or service that it has to only hold back a small percentage of its product from the market to cause a shortage that forces a disproportionate increase in prices for the product. One simple case might work like this: A company called Thingamajig, Inc. manufactures fifty-percent of all of thingamabobs sold in the country and thingamabobs have only a short life expectancy before they must be replaced, so there is a fairly constant demand for thingamabobs. Thingamajig, Inc. either cuts its production or just increases its inventories of thingamabobs so that it supplies five percent fewer to the market. As a result of there being fewer thingamabobs available in the market than are needed, a minor shortage develops. The customers are willing to pay ten percent more for thingamabobs so all of the suppliers raise their prices by ten percent. Now Thingamajig, Inc. gets a ten percent increase price on 95 percent of the units it was selling before it created the shortage so it has total revenues about four-and-one-half percent greater than it had and it's competitors get a full ten percent increase in revenues. Before its competitors have a chance to increase production of thingamabobs, Thingamajig, Inc. starts slowly releasing the extra thingamabobs it had put into inventory, so that fairly quickly the supply and demand are back in balance. The customers have grown accustomed to the ten-percent higher price of thingamabobs so the prices are unlikely to drop back unless there is an oversupply in the market. That's not likely to happen because Thingamajig, Inc.'s competitors didn't have enough time to buy more manufacturing equipment to be able to increase their production of thingamabobs before Thingamajig, Inc. filled the gap in the supply.

Although the above is a ridiculous example of what market power is, it gives the general idea. There are many situations that develop in free markets that cause the demands for products to outstrip supply and drive prices up, which have nothing to do with market power. Shortages do not always mean that one of the competitors has deliberately manipulated the supply to increase prices. In almost all cases, shortages and price increases, and oversupplies and price drops are the natural perturbations of the free markets which keep them in balance.

In any free market "reserves" adequate to meet any extreme demand are contrary to the supply-demand-price interactive balance. In a free market if there is never a shortage there will never be an increase in production. The concept of having reserves in a free market is like calling for a blitz and quarterback-sacking play in the Swan Lake Ballet. In a free market, any reserves from the prehistoric days of regulation will be absorbed and disappear to be replaced with the supply, demand, and price balance. That is unless there is an unnatural prescription for reserves by some regulatory body.

Unlike in the other free markets, shortages in the electric power market will cause extreme hardship for everyone because everyone needs electric power in every aspect of their daily lives. Whenever a shortage develops in the electric power industry there will be a general outcry for the heads of any and all suppliers in the market. Claims that the shortages stem from undue market power and from suppliers withholding power from the market will be the rule rather than the exception.

California and it's natural gas market provides a good example what is likely to develop in the electric power market. California recently experienced a shortage of natural gas and true to form, claimed that El Paso

Corporation was holding gas from the market to drive up prices. The California lawyer on a TV news special called *Blackout* said he had proof that El Paso was holding back gas and showed a chart of El Paso's own data which showed that its gas transmission service, which brings gas to the California border, was not running at full capacity. This of course meant to the lawyer that El Paso was withholding gas because, in the mind of a litigator, things happen only because manipulative corporations choose for them to happen. In actuality, the only conclusion which can be drawn from the fact, that a transmission facility is not operating to full capacity, is that the line is not carrying the maximum amount of product that it can physically handle. There are many reasons a transmission facility may not be carrying it's maximum capacity, the most likely of which is that no one called for enough product to push the transmission facility to its full capacity.

I seriously doubt that El Paso turned away customers who wished to buy gas, especially since they put the transmission-capacity and demand data out for everyone to see. One normally tries to hide data that would show it acted in bad faith. Knowing California's long history of resisting new development, new transmission facilities, new exploration for resources and new production facilities, it's more likely that California's infrastructure was not capable of using or handling as much gas as El Paso could supply.

Here's a simple example that may clarify the likely gas shortage situation in California. Assume there is a farmer in the Central Valley who is trying to grow watermelons on seventy-acres of prime Central Valley soil. He has two very long garden hoses and two farmhands who walk around watering the seventy-five-acre melon patch. Of course it's impossible to provide enough water for seventy-acres of melons from two garden hoses and, in the heat of the summer, all of the melon vines die and the farmer loses all of his melon crop. What does he do? He hires a lawyer and the lawyer sues the water company of course. You see the lawyer can prove that the ten-inch water main that supplies the farm has the capacity to provide up to a thousand gallons of water per minute at full capacity. Since the water company's own data shows that the water main was only carrying twenty gallons per minute, it's a fact that the water company was operating the water main at only two-percent of capacity and therefor was withholding water from the farmer's melon fields. In the litigators' mind his case is clear, the water company is guilty; it's perfect logic in the mind of a litigator who doesn't have to deal with reality but only public perception and misconception.

Who Should You Buy Power from
if You Have the Choice?

If in your state or market area you have the option of which generating company to purchase from then you may as well purchase from the generating company with the lowest rates. This is because, in the power market, the power you actually receive may have been generated by another company and there is no difference in quality or value of the energy you receive. If you buy from the generating company with the lowest reserve margin that's doing the worst job of maintaining its generating equipment and your generating company ends up causing a widespread power outage in your region, you will be affected no more and no less than all the other customers of all the other generating companies. All customers are similarly affected when the power system is ailing or dysfunctional regardless of how carefully they select their power supply company or how expertly or well their power supply company performs. It's sort of like the cabins aboard the HMS Titanic; when the ship sank the first class cabins, the lower class cabins and the sleeping areas down in steerage level of the ship all wound up on the sea floor together.

What You Can Do When the Blackouts Come

There's an old saying "If you want it done right do it yourself." In the free power market, when the capacity reserves or transmission capacity becomes insufficient to keep the lights on, customers will be forced to provide their own electric power reliability or suffer through the blackouts. The means customers choose to ensure their own electric reliability will depend on their needs for uninterrupted electric power, the kinds of discomforts and disruptions they are willing to accept, their local electrical and noise limit codes, and their financial resources.

Of course as with all shortcomings in our system the citizens living on the economic edge of our economy will have no options and will have to suffer just one more hardship. There's no way those having to live in subsidized housing, our older Americans on fixed incomes, or those who can just about meet the expenses for their basic needs will be able to pay for the electric reliability that was assured under the old regulated electric power system. They will just have to learn to live with blackouts.

Apples and Oranges
The Cost of Regulated Versus
Deregulated Electric Power

The proponents of deregulation claim that the cost of electric service will drop in the future because deregulation and competition force lower prices. It will be a difficult assessment to make if the federal government follows its current path of allowing generating companies to shed their responsibility for providing reliable electric service to all their customers under worst-case conditions.

If under deregulation, it is the customers who must provide their own backup facilities to contend with blackouts, then when the pre-deregulation cost of power is compared to the post-deregulation cost of power the customers' cost of providing their own post-deregulation electric reliability must be added to their electric costs in order to make a valid comparison.

Likely a whole new method of providing electric reliability will emerge under deregulation. Since there will be a class of customers who need and are willing to pay for the same degree of reliability that they have had in the past, the local transmission and distribution company, or a franchised non-affiliated private financial institution, will arrange to install back up generation facilities at the customer's site for a fixed periodic payment fee. In

California, such a market is in the early stages of development; remember, I said earlier that as goes California so goes the rest of the nation. By the time the rolling blackouts migrate east of the Mississippi River, there will be a number of entrepreneurial California firms who will be ready to jump into the blackout fracas with an offer we can't refuse. It is such entrepreneurial daring-do that will create a tremendous market for the residential and small-business generator and fuel cell backup systems.

Investing in small generator and fuel cell backup manufacturing companies will likely yield high returns, but only if the federal government continues its electric-deregulation-hands-off policy. If the federal government were to finally grasp the reality that mandatory capacity reserve margins are the only way to ensure a reliable electric power supply for the nation, and were to mandate such reserves, the need and market for residential backup systems would quickly evaporate.

Backup Power Supplies

There are a number of different kinds of backup power supply systems that can be used on site to provide electrical power to a house or commercial building in the event of a power system failure. Some are useful for supplying power for short periods while others can be used for extended periods or even indefinitely.

Portable generators – Portable generators are available from any number of equipment suppliers and they come in a wide variety of capacities and use a wide range of fuels. The majority of portable electric generating units are available in capacities from 2.7 kilowatts to 10 kilowatts and are fueled with gasoline. Such units cost anywhere from $500 to $1,800[2]. There are a number of larger units available in the 8-kilowatt to 13-kilowatt capacity range which will operate interchangeably on gasoline, propane, or natural gas. Some of these units can even have their fuel sources switched while they are running and connected to load. These generators are more expensive, with discounted prices ranging from about

---

[2]   All prices are the lowest from major equipment retailers offered in mail-order catalogs which are about 30-percent to 50-percent less than manufacturers' suggested maximum retail prices. Prices from retail stores can be significantly higher.

$1,900 to $2,800[3]. Like all internal combustion engine driven equipment portable generators produce exhaust noise. Some are more noisy than others. Some have quite good mufflers and are relatively quiet. Be aware that noise may be a factor in your or your neighbors' comfort. In selecting units you should keep fuel availability in mind. Most portable generators can run about 6 to 10 hours without refueling. It may be inconvenient and dangerous to store too much gasoline at your home, and all fuel should be stored in approved containers. In an extended blackout condition, remember that gas stations will not be able to supply gasoline unless they have their own electric backup systems because their pumps, computers, cash registers, etc. are operated on electricity.

Non-Portable Generators – There are a number of fully housed self-contained backup/standby natural gas or propane generation systems available for home use which are very price competitive. Guardian systems by Generac are the most popular and come with remote-mounted automatic transfer switches and controls to automatically exercise the generator by running it for a few minutes every week or every other week. The units cost from $2,000 - $3,500 for 6 - 13 kilowatt natural-gas/propane fueled, air-cooled systems running at 3,600 rpm to $5,400 - $10,000 for 15 - 45 kilowatt water-cooled systems running at 1,800 rpm.

---

[3] http://www.northerntool.com, http://www.norwall.com

Larger Non-Portable Diesel-Powered Generators - They are suitable for supplying small businesses and apartment buildings and designed for continuous duty service. Such units are available in capacities ranging from 15 Kilowatts to hundreds of kilowatts. A15-kilowatt low-speed (1,800 rpm) unit will cost about $8,000. Such a unit comes in its own enclosure which is fairly large, being about 6 feet long, three feet wide and about four-and-one-half feet tall. A unit such at this isn't designed only for back up service, but can serve as the exclusive source of continuous power for a remote site.

Residential Generators - For the most part residential customers will need only a little generating capacity to get by during blackouts. The basic energy requirements of the average home can be supplied by a small portable electric generator. A four or five-kilowatt portable generator will provide enough capacity to run a number of lights, a refrigerator, a freezer, a television, a computer and, at selected times, a microwave oven. Typically electric appliances draw the following loads:

incandescent light	100 watts
refrigerator	500 watts to run but
	1,200 watts to start
freezer	500 watts to run but
	1,200 watts to start
television	200 watts
computer	300 watts
microwave oven	1,000 watts

To supply three incandescent lights and one of each of the other items on the list would require a constant power supply of 2.8 kilowatts. However, it requires an extra 1,400 watts to start the refrigerator and freezer at the same time so that a generator with a capacity of 4.2 kilowatts would cover every possible eventuality. One would expect that the chances would be slim that a refrigerator and separate food freezer would both start simultaneously, however it is very likely if the electric power has been off for any period in excess of fifteen minutes. This is because both the refrigerator and food freezer would absorb enough heat over the period that they were not running so that their internal thermostats would be switched on, calling for their compressors to run. You should turn off the circuit breakers for electric appliances which cycle on automatically such as electric water heaters and air conditioners so the generator won't be inadvertently overloaded. Some electric water heaters have one heating element which draws about 3.5 kilowatts of power and some have two heating elements and can draw up to 7 kilowatts of power. Room-size air conditioners can draw up to 2 kilowatts of power and central air conditioning units can draw up to 6 kilowatts of power. If you plan to use a generator to supply the larger loads such as electric hot water heaters, air conditioners, heat pumps, electric baseboard heat or forced-air electric resistance furnaces (which can draw 25 kilowatts or more) you need to consult an electric power specialist who can give you professional advice on sizing a generating system or can design the best system for your needs.

If you plan to use a generator to get you through rotating or extended blackouts, your household electrical service must be modified by a licensed electrician to provide a dedicated electrical outlet for plugging in the generator and a cutout switch that disconnects the main service in your house from the outside electrical service drop, whenever the dedicated generator outlet is switched to receive power from the generator. You should acquire a portable generator capable of supplying power at 220 volts and have the electrician install a 220-volt generator outlet that matches the generator's 220-volt plug design and install a cut-out switch for 220-volts and a circuit breaker or fuse box with enough amperage to handle the maximum size generator you ever expect to connect to the circuit. Some of the non-portable natural gas and propane backup systems I mentioned above come with such remote cutoff switches which must be installed by a licensed electrician.

The national electric code requires that if you use an electric power supply in your home, such as an electric generator, fuel cell electric generator, or battery backup power supply, you must install a cut-off switch in the circuit that will disconnect the household circuits from the main power supply drop from the outside because, if you don't, your generator is going to be trying to serve electrical loads outside your house, which it doesn't have capacity to handle. In addition, if your generator is connected to and energizing the utility's distribution and transmission system (which is unlawful), you could kill an unsuspecting electric company worker working on the transmission lines or a neighbor or electrician in your neighbor's house who thinks the electrical service he is working on is not energized. You must realize that a 110-volt or 220-volt generator connected to your household circuits will provide whatever voltage is on the transmission system that supplies your house. If the transmission or distribution line serving your house is a 39- thousand volt line, then the 110-volt or 220-volt electricity you put on your household circuit from the generator, fuel cell or backup battery system will travel out to the transformer and will be stepped up to 39 thousand volts and will energize the distribution and transmission lines serving your residential area.

Any form of backup electric power, if not installed in accordance with the national electric code and operated with common sense, can be as deadly as a loaded gun and should be used and handled with equal respect.

Commercial Generators -Commercial electric customers will have greater capacity demands than residential customers and often will need to have their back up or reserve capacity come on line automatically when no one is around to oversee the operation of the equipment. There is a lot of large generation equipment available to meet the needs of any size commercial electrical need. Anyone needing to acquire generation backup for commercial applications needs to have a registered professional engineer design the system from the ground up. Often the equipment suppliers can furnish such design needs and can serve as general contractor to have the equipment installed.

All back up systems need to be tested and operated periodically to assure their availability when they will be needed, but this is especially true for the larger commercial units for which assured reliability is more critical than for household backup systems.

Battery Backup Systems - Battery backup systems, consisting of industrial batteries and DC/AV 120 Volt invertors, are available in all sizes from units which will only power a few lights to systems capable of supplying the full load of a house for 7 or 8 hours or more, depending on how much one wants to spend on batteries. A complete ready-to-install 120-volt system, including breaker, disconnect/bypass switch, 2 invertor/chargers, a panel box, and 4 industrial batteries capable of providing a combined 315 amp hours at 115 volts after inversion, will provide a peak capacity of 11 kilowatts and 34.65 kilowatt hours of energy. This system can provide the full needs of an average size home for about 6 to 12 hours. This size battery backup system would cost about $12,000[4]. The batteries when used in regular duty service will generally last 8 to 12 years.

The drawbacks of battery systems are the batteries are very cumbersome and heavy, and must be kept out of the elements, yet be well ventilated because they produce highly explosive hydrogen gas when charging. In addition if you ever have to dispose of the batteries, they are considered hazardous waste and may cost several hundred dollars each to have disposed. While battery backup systems are silent they are much more expensive, cumbersome, and dangerous than generator systems. They have the limitation of providing only a fixed amount of

---

[4]   http://www.traceengineering.com

energy before having to be recharged. A generator-powered system will provide energy so long as it can be fueled. A 12-kilowatt multi-fuel generator system, as described under residential systems above, would provide the same level of service as the 11-kilowatt battery backup system described but would cost only one quarter as much ($2,800).

Fuel Cell Electric Power Generation - Fuel cell generation technology is a byproduct of the space industry. Fuel cells which generate electric power from the combination of carbon and oxygen, while passing through a catalyst fluid or membrane, were developed for space vehicles. They produce almost no pollution in the form of nitrogen oxides or sulfur oxides but, like all fossil fueled systems, produce carbon dioxide, which doesn't promote significant global warming, in spite of all you may have heard from the concerned scientists whose research has been highly subsidized by the nuclear power industry for decades.

Fuel cell technology is just now reaching the commercial stage for residential size units. Large (very big) fuel cell generating systems have been used for years at hospitals, industrial plants and by communications companies for their remote communication sites.
The units can be fueled with either propane or natural gas.

Plug Power, a joint venture with General Electric and a number of other companies in the fuel cell development business has developed a fuel cell unit that's about the size of a heat pump and will provide the full needs of a home[5]. The units are supposed to be available for installation by licensed distributers in early 2002 and will cost from \$10,000 to \$15,000 depending upon size. They are totally silent and can be set up to provide hot water for heating or hot water for household use which increases the overall efficiency of the fuel consumption significantly. It appears from current costs for natural gas and propane that the fuel cost for the energy (neglecting the capital cost of the unit itself) would be in the 15 to 20 cents per kilowatt hour range.

The fuel cell units have almost no moving parts and require about \$200 per year maintenance and \$650 major component replacement every five or six years. The predictions are that after the units are in full production for four years the prices will drop to about \$3,000 - \$4,000 which will make them highly competitive with engine-powered generators, if the projections are correct. At that point, they would be much more desirable than engine-powered generators because of their simplicity, silence and reliability.

While Plug Power seems to be a bit ahead of the competition (and there are many competitors at various stages of commercial development in the field) H Power [6]is right behind Plug with a residential unit similar to Plug's to be commercially available within the year following Plug. See, competition really works without controls for some commodities and products.

---

[5]   http://www.plugpower.com

[6]   http://www.hpower.com

H Power reports that there was a bill introduced in congress on March 28, 2001 which proposed a $1,000 per kilowatt tax credit for purchasers of stationary fuel cell systems that supply home electricity. The bill was sponsored by Representatives Nancy L. Johnson (R-CT) and Michael R. McNulty (D-NY). Any tax incentive would only help to make fuel cells more economically competitive with engine powered generation. However I question whether the incentive would be a tax credit (a direct payment of $1000) or a income exemption in which $1,000 per kilowatt is exempted from tax — a real saving of about $300 per kilowatt. Even a $300 credit would be great because it would drop the effective cost of the first residential units from the $10,000 to $15,000 range down to the $7,000 to $12,000 range.

The only drawback I can see to the fuel cell systems is the possibility of an increase in fuel cost and a decrease in fuel availability. The generation companies are proposing to install only natural-gas-fueled combined-cycle combustion turbine generation units in the future and have been doing so for the last three or four years. The sudden sharp increase in natural gas usage in the electric generation industry has seriously stressed natural gas transmission services and we have seen just what that has done to the price of natural gas on the open market. Unless the natural-gas transmission lines gas can be expanded significantly and very quickly, the prices of natural gas will make the fuel cells and natural gas fueled engine generators for home use less attractive and make gasoline fueled units more desirable.

The problem with a free electric power market is that it's so dynamic that any economical decision you make today may be uneconomical next month. It's the same dilemma facing the large electric generating companies. It's easy to see why they are so reluctant to make any kind of commitment to building any new capacity.

Part 2

Black Start 2005
A novella premised on a dark, deregulated future

Chapter 1

The Channel 7 news studio is a brightly-lit stage. The actors, wired with hearing-aid-style earphones and miniature microphones read their lines from TELEPROMPTERS under the bright lights. Dozens of technicians scurry about in the foreground among the shadows, moving and focusing massive television cameras, and reading directions from their clipboards. In a massive soundproof glass-fronted control room overlooking the stage, six controllers direct the action.

Jim Stepe and Elaine Mercer are on stage with the Channel 7 logo centered on the fake wall behind them. The two smile into the active camera, trying their best to befriend their viewing public. They know which camera is currently active by the tiny red light-emitting diode beside the lens. It flashes every two seconds on the active camera. Behind every lens are thousands of curious minds soaking up the audio and visual information that radiates out of their television sets.

"Man oh man is it ever hot out there," Jim says, looking to Elaine for a response.

"The current temperature is ninety-seven degrees," she answers, reading from the TELEPROMPTER just above the active camera's lens. "I walked down to the deli for lunch and the soles of my shoes melted and stuck to the pavement while I was waiting to cross the square."

"This is supposed to be a news show, Elaine. You have to report the facts, no exaggerations, just the facts. If I go out to the corner will I find little puddles of melted shoe sole on the sidewalk?" Jim looks from Elaine to the camera, chuckles, and looks back to Elaine.

"Okay, Jim, I may have been exaggerating, but only a little."

Jim turns back to the camera. "We have a public service report from the people at Contran, and it's no exaggeration. They say that the air-conditioning loads are straining their system capacity. Everyone should turn off as many appliances as possible so they don't have to resort to brownouts and rotating blackouts to prevent a total blackout. Everyone, except those over the age of seventy or those who have severe respiratory disease, should turn their air conditioners off; don't just turn the thermostats up, turn the air conditioners totally off."

Chapter 2

About five miles south of the border between New York and Connecticut, George Tower is sitting on his couch in the dingy little living room of his small garden apartment. His stocking feet are propped on the naugahyde-covered footstool. George is fifty-six, divorced, and retired. His wife Liz left him three years before when he was still a climbing engineer/manager with the power company. He had little time for a home life and his wife had little use for an absentee husband. He had let her keep their magnificent home in Southern Connecticut and moved just across the New York state line as an expression of independence.

George's small apartment is painted eggshell white, although the greasy meals he cooks have colored the kitchen ceiling and walls a yellowish tan. There are no pictures, paintings, or any other adornments on the walls.

He never imagined that he'd have to spend a significant amount of time in the apartment but he also never imagined that he would fall from grace at the power company and be effectively relegated to obscurity, as one of America's fixed income retirees. He has a bottle of beer in his left hand and the TV remote in his right. He's a bitter rejected relic of the old regulated electric power system.

He flips through the channels and stops when he sees Elaine Mercer's face. He concludes that she is sexy but has an innocent girl-next-door look. Elaine's TV-framed face speaks. "We haven't had a total regional blackout since November 1965 and that was in mild weather. That blackout brought down the whole northeast coast from Delaware to Canada for almost a day. If you are too young to remember, then take my father's word for it; it was inconvenient. I can't remember it, being only 29 years old."

Jim smiles broadly. "Nor me . . . don't remember a thing about it." Jim's puts on his totally-honest-reporter face and looks deep into the camera lens. "We're all less than thirty here at Channel 7."

Elaine laughs. "That's righ . . ."

The picture on George's TV slams down to a pinpoint on a black screen at the same time the lamp on the end table goes out. The only light in the small room is coming in through the milky grime on the window pane beside the TV.

"Damnation!" George gets up and makes his way across the small room, heading for the kitchen pantry. His big left toe slams into the leg of a kitchen chair that's out of place. "Oh, shit . . . damnation, oh." He leans against the kitchen doorframe, takes the last swig of beer from his bottle and tosses the bottle into the enameled sink where it smashes, sending shards of glass across the kitchen counter and stove top. "Shit, shit, and more shit!"

He feels for a drawer handle, finds it, and pulls the drawer open. His fingers dance through papers and unidentifiable objects until they detect the round barrel of a flashlight. The light comes on and the yellow ellipse of blinding brightness moves along the wall to the pantry.

George hobbles to the pantry and on a shelf, behind some cans of peas and corn, he finds the portable radio. He takes the radio back into the living room, where he puts it on the coffee table, places the lighted flashlight beside it, and sits back onto the couch. He turns on the radio and it greets him with waterfall sounds—total static. He turns the tuner dial and a man's voice jumps from the radio.

". . . . so bad. According to our callers, it seems that power is out everywhere, at least everywhere our listeners are. Now we'll find out just how far our listeners can hear us. If there's anyone out there who still has lights give us a call at area code (212) 555-1067. We've heard stories that the problems started out in Ohio and Michigan early this afternoon. A friend of mine at WZBX in Shelby called me about two-thirty and said there were problems with brownouts and rotating blackouts all over Ohio and up into Michigan. This can't be part of that, can it?"

The DJ's assistant and straight man raises his hand on the other side of the soundproof glass in the adjacent monitoring room and nods.

"We have a caller from Wakefield, Rhode Island on the line. Hello, Wakefield!"

"Hello, New York."

"This is the Hairman at WJRG, that's Jerg radio ninety-two-point-six.. Who do I have on the Line?"

"This is Jason Mason."

"That's quite a handle, Jason, but didn't my assistant tell you not to use your last name?"

"Yeah, sorry, I forgot."

"Do you still have power in up there in Rhode Island?"

"Yes."

"Where are you Jason?"

"I'm in Wakefield."

"Come on Jason, get with the program will you? Are you in your home, in a phone booth, in the Rhode Island state pen or what?"

"Oh, I'm in the bar at Iggy Palmasano's restaurant."

"Does everyone in the bar there listen to Jerg radio 92?"

"No. I happened to pick you up on my car radio just as I was pulling into the restaurant parking lot. I called you as soon as I got inside. Oh, hell!"

"Watch your language Jason or my assistant's going to have to bleep you. What are you 'oh helling' about? Or should I ask?"

"You shouldn't ask, but if you do I'll tell you that the lights just went out."

"You heard it first here, America, on Jerg radio ninety-two-point-six. The lights just went out in Rhode Island. Jason, how is everyone there in the bar taking it? Jason? Jason are you there?"

Jim's assistant shakes his head from side to side and brings the edge of his right hand across his throat.

"Well, New York, Jason in Wakefield, Rhode Island has dropped off the edge of the earth. Or maybe he's okay and it's we who have just dropped off the edge of the earth."

George slumps down further on the couch and leans his head back against the cushion.

"Well Contran, is this the blackout you said wasn't coming? We're in deep shit now."

Chapter 3

Contran's central-dispatch control room looks like a military battle headquarters. Twenty-five men and women sit at consoles punching data into keyboards and looking alternatively from their personal cathode-ray monitors to the big-board. On the back-lit big-board are almost a hundred lines of different colors representing various voltage transmission lines connecting various transmission and distribution substations. Five, no, now six of the lines are flashing yellow.

Carlton Hayes, the shift manager, is standing on a balcony overlooking the control room. "Come on people," he shouts, "you have got to drop some more load and fast or we're going to lose another one and we can't afford to lose even one more."

Audrey Calhoon, a young woman shouts from her console on the control floor, "I've got to trip thirty-seven ... the three-fifty-kV line from Murtaugh to Cunningham. It's more than fifty degrees above design max. It's going to sag all the way to the ground or pull apart if I don't take it off line. Then when we won't have it to help us get back if the whole beast goes south on us!"

Hayes shouts back immediately, "The chairman of the board's mansion is in Cunningham. If we drop his area we'll all be out on the street."

Audrey purses her lips. Her eyes betray her hatred. "We need to get past the internal politics and start making decisions that make sense!"

"Watch your attitude little lady or I'll fire your collegiate little ass."

"You won't be able to if we don't save this system right here and now. Your fat management ass will be out the door before mine."

"Miz Calhoon, you're fired!"

"Fine!" Audrey pushes back from the console in her roller-wheeled chair. She stands up, stretches, and with her hands in the air, throws her boss the double-barreled bird. "Screw you!"

"God damn it! Get back to your post!" Carlton Hayes shouts.

"I thought you fired me."

"I did but not effective until the end of your shift."

"Screw you again. If I'm fired, I'm fired now, not whenever you think it may be convenient."

"Sit down damn it! You're not fired but you will get a reprimand in your personnel file!"

Audrey continues on her feet, "I hate to bring the subject up again but if we don't drop thirty-seven we're going to end up pulling the whole thing down around our ears. If that happens we'll be in a black-start crisis and we'll all be out on the street."

"Okay, okay already, pull thirty-seven!"

The flashing line on the big-board that represents line thirty-seven stops flashing and is suddenly covered with short red crosshatched lines.

Audrey announces to the room, "Too late, we just lost it. In this business you don't get a second chance to make the right decision." She sits back down and rolls her chair back into position behind her monitor. Under her breath, to her neighbor, she says, "He's the worst side effect of the whole damn deregulation debacle."

Her coworker winks. "Don't you know? He's going to show us how to save money."

"Yeah, how much do you think that genius just saved the company when line thirty-seven melted down?"

"Good point."

On the big board three more lines start flashing in red rather than yellow and another transmission line starts flashing yellow. Audrey shouts, "The system is going unstable. We're getting voltage spikes and dips all over the place. The breakers on fifty-nine, forty-six and twenty-three just popped and the no-load condition on Murtaugh steam plant must have caused it to over-speed. It just tripped off-line."

A man stands up at his console and runs his hands through his thinning hair. He says in a matter-of-fact tone of resignation, "The whole system is going down. It's just too unstable. All the transient voltages are tripping the protection relays and taking all of our biggest lines out of service."

"Is there any way to save it?" Carlton Hayes shouts the question over the growing sound of murmuring from the people at their consoles.

"No chance in hell at this point," Audrey shouts up at the balcony. "We're heading for a total blackout."

"We can't. If we go totally down it could take two days to get the whole system back up and running."

"We can and we are. We'll finally get that chance to test our emergency black start plan."

Audrey's neighbor says, "That's a test I can well do without."

"It's a test we can all do without. I bet it's three days before we get any sleep again." Audrey purses her lips. "There goes my hot date tonight. I can't believe it. The guy could be a Chippendale Dancer and I'm going to stand him up. Oh God I hate this job."

Chapter 4

Emma Lou Hastings fidgets with the sheets on her husband's bed. "It's okay Henry. The power's out but the batteries will keep your respirator running. It was designed for just this sort of thing."

Henry puts on his face of understanding and acceptance. He wants to put his wife of fifty-two years at ease. Maybe it's good that she doesn't understand just how serious the power outage really is.

Before the market became totally competitive, blackouts were local affairs and were most often caused by a maintenance failure or on oversight. Henry had worked for the power company for thirty-five years and fully appreciates the differences between the blackout they are now experiencing and those of the past. He's glad Emma doesn't understand because if she did she'd be in a panic and he's not up to dealing with her panic and his probable demise.

The respirator's batteries will last about eight hours and after that it will stop and he will expire unless someone can bring in some fresh batteries or set up a portable generator at the house. It was three weeks ago yesterday that he decided to come home and not spend another minute at that sterile hospital with it's sterile nurses and orderlies. The hospital is highly attractive to him at the moment; it has a five-megawatt-fuel-cell electric backup power system.

"Emma, I want you to call George Tower. His number is in my little phonebook on the desk."

"Who is he?"

"You, know. He's the guy I worked with on that Billby Plant outage investigation about ten years back."

"A Contran engineer?"

"No. He was pushed out last year... didn't see eye-to-eye with the new management."

"Oh, one of the good guys?"

"Yes, Emma, he's one of the good guys."

"In that case I'll call him. What am I supposed to be calling about?"

"You're not calling him about anything, I am. Just dial him and bring me the walk-around phone."

Emma goes into the den. She puts on her reading glasses. She finds Henry's little phone book on the desk. She thumbs through the pages and finds George Tower under the *G's*.

"Wouldn't you know it?" She mumbles.

She dials the number on the regular telephone. She can't stand dialing numbers on a handset. George answers right away.

"Mr. Tower?" She asks.

"Yes, this is George Tower."

"Mr. Tower you don't know me but I'm Henry Hastings wife, Emma. He asked me to dial you."

"Well, I'll be. How's the old son of a gun?"

"He's fine. Not really fine . . . his lungs are failing . . . but other than that he's fine. If you hold on for a moment, I'll take him the phone. You just hold, okay?"

"Sure, I'll hold, no problem."

Emma picks up the walk-around phone and turns it on. She then hangs up the *real* telephone. "You still there, Mr. Tower?"

"Yes, I'm still with you."

Emma takes the walk-around to Henry, carrying it like she would carry a wet puppy.

"Thank you Emma."

Henry speaks into the handset. "Say, is that you, George?"

"It's me, Henry. What are you up to these days?"

"Oh I just lay around here sucking air out of a machine, watching my wife play step-and-fetch-it for me."

"Sounds like a rough life. When you retired you went all the way, huh?"

"How are you taking to retired life, George?"

"I'm not retired, Henry, I was fired."

"You were Retired. They gave you a healthy buyout didn't they?"

"Yeah but it was just a bribe to leave quietly, so they wouldn't have to fire me."

"You always were a stickler for the details."

Henry puts his hand over the mouthpiece of the walk-around phone. "Emma, don't you have things to do? You don't have to hang around here. I'll be okay."

Emma gives him a dirty look. "I can take a hint."

"You can stay if you like, I just thought you might like a minute to yourself and I'm busy on the phone and won't need anything for a few minutes at least."

Emma walks out speaking over her shoulder. "I do have some darning I'd like to get to."

Henry removes his hand from the mouthpiece. "Sorry about that, George. I had to talk to the little woman a moment."

"Little woman? You're a real throwback, Henry. If you hadn't retired, they'd have fired you too, for not being politically correct."

"George, now that Emma left, I can talk. This is the big one you kept talking about isn't it?"

"It looks that way. It sounds like they can't close the circuits off quickly enough and can't isolate the outage. It just keeps growing."

"I was afraid of that. You know these people got complacent. They don't remember the Northeast Blackout of '65 or the New York blackout and riots of '77."

"Not many around who were around in '65 or '77 and fewer who were actually caught in the outages."

"Yeah, and if you haven't experienced it first hand, you don't appreciate just how bad it gets when all the power goes out. I need to talk quickly because, if my guess is right, it won't be long before the telephones go."

"I thought the telephone companies have their own backups."

"They do for their operation centers but there are too many stations out there that depend totally on the electric grid. The backups don't put out enough power to supply the whole phone system. The voltage will keep dropping down on the phone circuits until the communications switchgear doesn't work any longer."

"Well, you had better speak fast then. You never know when we'll lose our connection."

"The reason I called you George, is to ask a favor."

"Sure, anything I can do. I mean it, *anything*."

"I'm on a respirator. I called the hospital about moving back there but they say they're overcrowded and there's no way they can handle me. I've called everywhere and can't find a portable generator. The respirator has a battery backup good for about eight hours."

"After that?"

"After that I'm a goner unless someone can get more hulking batteries or a portable generator in here."

"It's done, Henry. Don't worry. I'll get you a generator."

"Thanks, George. I don't want Emma to start getting worried five or six hours from now when the power's still not back on."

"I understand and don't worry. You're still on Euclid Street aren't you?"

"Yes, still here . . . 2315 Euclid."

"I'm glad you called me, Henry."

"So am I, George. So am I."

"I'm going to hang up now so I can see about rounding up a generator. Hang tight."

"I'm hanging. . . don't know how tight but I'm hanging."

"Take care, Henry."

"You too, George, and thanks again."

"Sure, bye."

George gently hangs up the telephone. Deep in thought, he scratches his forehead. Now where in the hell am I going to find a portable generator this far into a blackout?

Chapter 5

Carlos and Maria Managua sit in total darkness on the tiled floor of the elevator. Maria weeps quietly and Carlos does his best to console her as he counts, "Tres minutos. . . uno, dos, tres, cuatro. . ."

Maria cries out, "Aquí viene otra vez!"

Carlos holds his wife tightly as the contraction builds. After thirty seconds of suffering with what feels like a massive Charlie horse in her gut, Maria finally relaxes, "Ahhh."

Carlos laments, "We've got to get out of here or Josè will be born in this elevator."

"You mean Elise, don't you?"

"Josè. Él será un muchacho."

"Elise, una muchacha . . . a girl."

"We'll see," Carlos teases.

"I don't want no stupid boy. Uno is enough."

"What are you talking about? We don't have a boy."

"You Carlos. You are not a man. You are a little boy. I told you don't use the elevator after the lights go out and come back on but no, you say everything will be fine. Let's use the elevator, you say. It will be mucho faster you say. Why are men . . . little boys so stupido?"

"Si, si, I was wrong. The lights come back in a minuto. We be at the hospital in no time."

"Your testículos tell you that?"

"Maria, I know you are hurting and mad but don't be so mean."

"It's not bad enough that you make me suffer through neuve months of throwing up in the toilet every morning? You make me have the baby on the floor of a dirty, hot, stuffy elevator?"

This is not my kind and loving wife. This is some vicious female hormone monster. "Can anybody out there hear me?" Carlos shouts up at the ceiling of the elevator.

"Hello," comes a very faint reply. Dean Collins is standing in the fifteenth-floor hallway of the old apartment building. He's holding a lighted candle.

"We're in the elevator and my wife's having a baby. Can you help us?"

"I don't know. How can I help?"

"Can you call the police or the fire department?"

"I'll try, just stay where you are."

"Don't worry, we won't go anywhere!" Under his breath Carlos says, "Idiot. Where the hell does he think we will go?"

"Oh, here it comes again, oh Holy Mother!" Maria clutches Carlos' arm to her chest and gasps for breath.

Chapter 6

The subway car is dark and some women and children are whimpering as several men work in the darkness to open one of the sliding doors.

"Shouldn't we just stay where we are?" One male voice asks.

"For how long? We could be here for days."

"Blackouts never last for more than an hour or so."

"I work for Contran, and believe me, this could last for days."

A menacing voice calls out in the darkness, "What say we kill the son of a bitch from Contran?"

Another male voice, "Sounds good to me!"

The man from Contran does not respond.

"Speak up, Mister Contran, so we will know where you are, Mister Contran."

A woman's voice joins the dialogue. She is nervous and very angry. Her husband told her just hours ago that he's leaving her for that young woman in his office. She's on her way to the bitch's apartment to put an end to it all. Her voice is high and strained. "Isn't that just like a bunch of dim-witted men? They get stranded, so do they want to work together to get out? No, they want to start a fight . . . kick each others' asses around in the dark."

"We can kick girls' asses just as easily." The male voice is totally defiant.

The woman has had her fill of macho, hyper-testosterone males. "Up yours needle dick. I've got a gun and I don't have to see your sorry ass to shoot it."

The defiant voice challenges, "Oh Christ. Just what we need, a woman with PMS and a gun!"

Blam! The subway car is bathed in a flash of white light. Everyone sees the afterimage of men and women frozen in time—their eyeballs having retained the snapshot of the scene when the gun discharged. The scene frozen in their eyeballs is contrary to what they hear—people moving about, scrambling for cover. The passengers continue to see the victim's frozen image and the frozen image of the woman with the flaring gun. The passengers blink quickly trying to get rid of the image burned onto the retinas of their eyeballs. They try in vain to see what's happening now. In the total darkness their efforts are futile; they continue to see the eerie afterimage flash of the violent past moment.

"Oh, God! I think she shot me . . . she did, she shot me. I'm bleeding!" The voice is coming from the direction of the muzzle-flash-frozen image of the man with a defiantly-raised middle finger.

Chapter 7

Milton Banes looks in his rearview mirror at the passenger in the cab's backseat. The well-dressed middle-aged gentleman is reading some kind of report resting in his lap. Milton wonders just how long he will wait before complaining. The traffic lights are out as far as he can see up Park Avenue. He knows as well as every other cabby in New York that the traffic will never move so long as the lights fail to function.

"What's the holdup?" comes the voice from the backseat.

"All of the traffic lights seem to be out. Traffic's not moving at all."

"I've got to get to the market for a meeting in a half-hour. Fifty bucks if you can get me there on time."

"A million bucks won't get you there on time. Traffic's not moving anywhere."

The gentleman laments, "This is a hell of a time for the traffic lights to go out," then goes back to his reading. A minute later, the cab's two-way radio crackles. Milton turns up the volume just enough to hear so it won't disturb his obviously well-to-do customer. He strains to hear the two-way conversation.

"Dispatch to eighty-two. Where are you?"

"Eighty-two here. I'ze at fifth and Park."

"Your regular four o'clock called. Wants to know why you're a half-hour late."

"You know the traffic lights are out?"

"Yeah, I know. There's a blackout all over the city."

"Then why are you callin' me, man."

"I just called to find out how traffic is moving."

"Well, traffic ain't. Nothing's gonna move 'til the lights come back on."

"Well have a good day eighty-two."

Milton calls back to his passenger. "The power is out all over the city. It's not just the traffic lights. I suspect that trading is suspended on the floor of the exchange too."

"What would a cabby, even a New York cabby, know about the stock exchange?"

"I trade in the market. What do you think, cabbies don't know how to make a buck?"

"I always knew you guys knew how to make a buck. I just never imagined you knew enough to invest one."

"A lot you know. Hell, every cabby I know has a 401K and an IRA."

"You're kidding, right?"

"No joke."

"What stocks are you holding?"

"Mostly new energy market stuff."

"Like what?"

"Like fuel cell development stocks."

"What would a cabby know about fuel cells?"

"Six months ago I sat for two hours in a traffic jam at the square. My passenger was an electrical engineer from Contran. He told me all about how we were heading for electric blackouts and how fuel cells for home use would become the best investments since the Internet stocks took the big tumble."

"That's just panic talk. Do you think the government would let the electric power industry get in bad shape?"

"Depends."

"Depends on what? On how much is in it for the big boys."

"You sound like those anti-government fanatics out in Idaho."

"You trust the big boys in DC to do what's best for you and me?"

"Sure, what's good for us, is good for the country and that's what gets them reelected."

"You sound like someone who's been to DC for a brainwash."

"You sound like someone who believes every nutcase who climbs into the backseat of your cab."

"I don't believe every nutcase. For example, you haven't said one thing that would convince me that you know anything about the electric power market."

"That's where you are totally wrong. I worked on Senator Rudlam's committee, you know, the one that looked into the state PUC's electric-power-deregulation initiative."

"Why doesn't that just fill me with confidence?"

"You obviously have a closed mind."

"I don't have a closed mind but I don't believe all the bull that our government feeds us either."

"But you believe some guy who rides in the back of your cab?"

"Sure, what he said about there not being enough generating capacity in the country made sense. Besides, the guy works for Contran so he should know."

"Contran has a lot people working for them. You're sure the guy wasn't a Contran janitor?"

"He wasn't a janitor and I'll put my fuel cell stocks up against anything you own. I'll bet you right now that they'll do better than anything you have."

"Yeah, right, and what makes you so sure?"

"This blackout . . . If this thing lasts just a few hours longer, my fuel cell stocks will go through the roof, that is, whenever the stock market opens again."

"You may be right. The American public isn't the most educated when it comes to the stock market and they do tend to get carried away with panic buying."

"Yeah and there's nothing that can panic people more that total darkness in New York. In fact, if the lights don't come on soon, I'm going to just walk home and leave the cab here."

"You can't just leave it here."

"And why not. You think it's going to block traffic?"

"Something may happen to it while you're gone. What if the cops have it towed?"

"I'll get it back."

"What if it's damaged?"

"It's not mine. It belongs to the company. They have insurance."

"It would make more sense if you stayed with your car."

"You don't have any idea of what it's like when the lights go out in New York, do you? This cab is not worth my life."

"I think you exaggerate a bit."

"Think so huh? You sit right here all night and I'll be back after sunup to identify your body. By the way, you missed your meeting."

The passenger looks at his watch. "Damn! I'd do better to walk."

"You're right about that. We've moved about ten feet in the last fifteen minutes."

"Okay, I'm outta here. How much do I owe you?"

The cabby pulls the meter flag down. "That'll be thirty-five bucks."

"That's a crime. Thirty-five bucks for about three blocks."

"It's a crime all right. I'll give you a receipt and you can send it to Contran for reimbursement."

"You think they'd pay it?"

"Hell no. They'll call this an act of God. You watch. They'll blame it on the weather or sunspots or the alignment of the planets. It will be anything but Contran's fault. This blackout will cost the city and the store owners and us a bundle but no one will get a dime. We'll get screwed and it will all be God's fault, you watch."

The gentleman hands a fifty-dollar bill over the seat. He glances at the driver registration card attached to the back of the front seat. "Here, Mr. Banes, keep the change. I think you're going to have a long unproductive day."

"Thanks . . . er . . . "

"Martin Walters."

"Thanks Mr. Walters. I enjoyed the conversation. Where are you from?"

"Originally, Yonkers."

"You're shitting me."

"I shit you not. I grew up in Yonkers. My father left when I was ten and my mother went a little strange two years later. She shipped me out to Philly when I was thirteen to live with my aunt. My mother never was right after that and I never came back. I ended up going to Penn State. This is the first I've ever been back . . . and wouldn't you know it, someone turns out the lights in my honor." He opens the rear door and gets out slowly.

"Good luck Marty. Don't forget to buy some fuel cell stocks as soon as the market opens, hopefully not for two days yet."

"I'll buy a few shares. I hope your stocks do well."

"Yeah, maybe if they do, I can send my boy to Penn State."

"I'll take that as a compliment. You know you're about the most savvy cab driver I've ever ridden with. We don't have any cabbies like you in Philly."

"I'll take *that* as a compliment. Be careful out there and, for God's sake, don't be out on the streets after dark. This isn't anything like Philly, believe me!"

Martin shuts the car door and steps up on the curb. "I'd say have a good day but I think it's too late for that."

"Take care." The cabby smiles and nods. "Wall Street is straight ahead, about twenty blocks. It'll take you 'bout forty-five minutes if you walk fast. I don't think anyone will be expecting you to show up for your appointment."

Martin nods in return and heads up the sidewalk. As he walks, he notices all of the frustrated drivers and passengers in the stalled cars and hears the blaring horns. Funny, he hadn't noticed the horns at all when he was in the cab.

Chapter 8

Johnny Capello is sitting with his mother on the front steps of their brownstone row house. They are wet with perspiration. The temperature is more than a hundred degrees in the shade and the asphalt pavement is so hot that pigeons can't walk across the street between the bumper-to-bumper cars without burning their feet.

Johnny is sixteen going on twenty-five. He's done it all. Well, done most of it, but he has seen the rest. Life in the Bronx is an education in itself. He has managed to stay out of jail by being just a bit smarter and faster than the average teenager.

Mrs. Capello is thirty-seven but she looks much older. It's the constant worry about her only child that has aged her. Unconditional love, that's what Father Robert says will save the younger generation from itself. Unconditional love, night after sleepless night may save the young, but it will likely kill their elders. Mrs. Capello wonders if her Johnny will ever grow into a responsible adult. Her greatest fear is that he will die without ever having the chance.

It was eighteen months ago that she gave up arguing with him about his lifestyle and his lowlife friends. Her constant complaining was driving him away and she knew he wouldn't last a month out on the streets on his own. AIDS, guns, knives—there are just too many ways to lose a son in this world.

Sitting on the top of the stoop with her feet on the next step down, Mrs. Capello brushes the wrinkles from her apron and then hugs her knees to her chest. "Would you like another PBJ sandwich?"

"Nah. You know I'm not into sandwiches."

"The power's out. You know I can't cook when the power's out."

"Yeah, I know, Mom. I think I'll head over to see what Juan's doin'."

"You know he's going to be up to no good. You shouldn't stay out after dark with the power out all over the city. No telling what's going to happen."

"It's a new experience, this blackout. My social studies teacher says we should reach out for new experiences. She says it's the way we grow."

"Your social studies teacher is a ding-a-ling. She doesn't know from anything. A young save-the-world twit from a highty-toighty town in Connecticut."

"She's a mighty fine-looking twit."

"Johnny! Be respectful of your elders, especially your teachers."

"I thought you said she was a doesn't-know-from-nothing, highty-toighty, save-the-world twit?"

"She it, but it doesn't matter. You still have to respect your elders. If you want to get anywhere in life you have to learn to show respect even when it isn't deserved. That's how you get ahead."

"I don't want to get ahead if I've got to respect my elders, even when they don't know shit."

"Don't talk like that. You know I don't like it."

"Sorry. But you know I'm not going to bow down and yes-sir and yes-ma'am idiots just because they were born a few years before me."

"Just learn to hold your tongue. If you can't say nothing nice then don't say nothing at all, my mother always used to say."

"And Grandpa used to say f-'em if they can't take a joke."

"Your grandpa was no kind of man to pattern yourself after."

"He's the only man I could pattern myself after."

"Don't give me that stuff about you needing your dad. That man was a totally useless bum and if I hadn't thrown him out you'd be heading for bum hood too."

"Maybe if he'd been around, I could have decided for myself what kind of man he was."

"He was a violent man. He learned it from his father. He wouldn't have put up with the stuff I've put up with from you. He'd have beat your head in."

"Maybe a beating would have done me some good."

"You're a real contrary one aren't you? If you think a beating would have done you good you should have told me earlier. Mr. Jameson, next door, is always saying you need a good beating. I'm sure he'd have been more than happy to come over and do it if I'd asked him."

"If that old fart had tried I'd 've knocked his teeth out."

"So you don't want a beating even if you know it would do you some good?"

"You're starting to piss me off, Mom. I'm going to go over to Juan's before I say something I shouldn't." Johnny stands up.

Mrs. Capello looks up at her son. There's disapproval in her dark eyes. "Maybe say something like *piss me off?*"

"Yeah, something like that."

"It'll be getting dark soon. You better take a flashlight."

"Good idea," Johnny picks up his empty glass tumbler, gets to his feet, pulls open the screen door and goes inside. "Won't you need the flashlight?"

"If you can get some batteries, there's an extra one on the top shelf of the pantry behind the box of vermicelli. It's been there for years."

Johnny comes out with the flashlight in hand. He unscrews the back and shakes out the batteries. "They're all corroded. You can't leave a flashlight for years with the batteries in it."

"Can you get some more?"

"I'll pick some up at G-Mart."

Mrs. Capello reaches into her apron pocket and pulls out a crumpled five-dollar bill, which Johnny eagerly accepts. He leans over and gives her a peck on the cheek.

Her eyes turn glassy. "Be careful. I love you."

"I love you too. Don't worry about me. I'll be fine. I'm a survivor."

"Everyone is a survivor until the day they die."

Johnny chuckles and shakes his head. "Sometimes you really surprise me. Everyone's a survivor until they die . . . I'll have to drop that one on Juan. He'll love it."

"I wasn't kidding. No one thinks anything bad will ever happen to them, but it does. Remember what your grandma always used to say."

"Never give a sucker an even break?"

"No. She said the unexpected always happens unexpectedly."

Johnny throws his head back and laughs without restraint. He finally stops laughing and works to catch his breath. "I think the saying is *Always expect the unexpected.*"

"Isn't that what I just said?"

"Yeah, sure, Mom." Johnny bounces down the front steps, turns and walks up the sidewalk. He looks over his shoulder to see his mother wipe the wetness away from the corners of her eyes with the tips of her fingers. When their eyes meet, she quickly pulls her hands away from her face and rests them in her lap. Johnny winks and she smiles happily. One of Johnny's winks can keep her going for a couple of weeks.

Johnny turns right after walking two blocks and enters the G-Mart which is two doors from the corner. Connie, arms crossed, is resting behind the cash register, her butt leaning against the glass counter behind her.

"The cash register doesn't work. The power's out," she repeats for the fiftieth time this hour.

"I know the power's out. I just need two D-size batteries for my flashlight." Johnny walks past her to the battery stand.

"The power's out and the cash register doesn't work."

He picks up a sealed plastic pack of two D batteries. "I heard you. I just need these batteries." He walks back to face Connie, the talking statue. He holds out the five-dollar bill.

She doesn't move. "The power's out the cash register won't work. I can't even open the cash drawer to make change."

"Take the five. Some day I'll come back for the change."

"I don't want your five dollars. Come back after the power's on."

"Call your manager. I'm sure he'll tell you to take the money."

"The phone quit working ten minutes ago. Come back after the power comes back on."

"After the power's on the streetlights will be on and I won't need the batteries, now will I?"

"Come back later."

"Are you going to take my money or not?"

"Not."

"Fuck you." He flips the bill at her and leaves. The bill flutters to the floor at her feet.

She ignores the bill on the floor by her right toe. "I'll tell the cops you lifted the batteries." Her words are flat, devoid of emotion.

"I'll tell the cops you've got your head up your ass." Johnny walks out, passing a woman entering the store with a baby in her arms.

As the door slowly closes behind him, Johnny hears, "The power's out and the cash register doesn't work."

"I need formula for my baby. I'm sure I have the correct change."

"Can't take your money. I can't open the cash register drawer, so I can't put your money in it."

Johnny now knows something he never suspected before. Power blackouts cause severe retardation.

Chapter 9

Elaine is looking tired, even with all her TV makeup. The thrill of the coverage is gone and the repetition is wearing on her nerves. The station has its own diesel generators and they are transmitting a TV signal, but who's watching? The only ones who could possibly be viewing are in the hospitals, police stations, firehouses and the few businesses and homes with backup generators. If every person who could watch were watching they would have fewer viewers than watched TV in New York the first month after television sets were first offered for sale by Sears Roebuck Company in the early fifties.

"The blackout has reached disastrous proportions. The streets are still wall-to-wall with abandoned cars. The mayor has declared an emergency and the National Guard is patrolling on the sidewalks in their jeeps. There are roving gangs of youths and older gangs breaking into businesses all over the city. None of the fire or burglar alarms without battery backups are working and there are so many of those going off that the police and fire departments are responding only to fire alarms and emergency injury calls. Some of the gangs have begun setting fire to some of the abandoned cars. Now we'll go to Tony Cochrane who is coming to us via a live feed from Times Square."

The screen of the monitor mounted in the glass top of the desk in front of Elaine fills with an eerie flickering reddish view of Times Square, like no one has seen it before. It's reminiscent of the TV news the station showed after night attacks by the Viet Cong in the late sixties. There are seven automobiles casting flickering firelight onto the familiar landmarks and the landmarks aren't the least bit familiar without their usual neon advertising. The camera pans away from the warlike scene to Tony Cochrane's talking head.

"It's unbelievable out here, Elaine. If I weren't sure I am awake I'd think I was having a nightmare. The destruction is horrendous. I don't think there's an unbroken window within ten blocks of where I'm standing."

The camera pans up the sidewalk behind him and there are all kinds of goods from inside the stores strewn along the concrete.

"There were three young men killed right here earlier." The camera pans down to two large dark areas on the sidewalk then up to a massive broken window frame. "A national guard spokesman reported that a team of three guardsmen ordered a large gang of teens to drop the items they were carrying out of that smashed window and two of the gang pulled guns and started firing on the guardsmen. According to the spokesman, the guardsmen fired in self defense but some stray bullets hit several others in the gang. The two young men who allegedly pulled guns were killed and three others had to be taken by helicopter to the trauma center at Elmhurst Hospital."

"How are those wounded young men doing, Tony?"

"Well, Elaine, according to the spokeswoman at Elmhurst, two are in guarded condition and the other is still in critical condition."

"Tony, the widespread blackout in sixty-five didn't result in such a disaster as we are now having. You're out there on the streets where it's all happening. Do you have any thoughts about why there's such a difference between now and then?"

"I'm not at all sure, Elaine, but I suspect that the youth of today have shorter fuses than the youth of the sixties. Remember, the youth back then had more to worry about."

"What do you mean, more to worry about?"

"Back then all the teenagers were facing going to Vietnam. A blackout probably didn't seem like such a big thing to them."

"How about all the abandoned cars, Tony?"

"It might be that there is a lot more traffic on the streets now and without streetlights the infrastructure probably just can't handle it."

"Well, Tony, thank you for your insights. Be careful out there."

"We'll be careful, Elaine. We're going to see if we can make it down to the United Nations building and have a report from there in an hour or so."

"That'd be great, Tony. Thanks for the fine report and we'll get back to you a bit later."

Elaine looks into the camera lens. "As you can see, it's a real disaster on the streets of New York. We're getting reports from Washington, D.C. that things aren't much better there. We understand that a large contingent of marines from Quantico, Virginia has been called in to set up a perimeter of protection around the White House. Of course the president is at his Kentucky White House retreat. We understand that the blackout covers almost all of the country east of the Mississippi River and stops at the Texas state line. We have Stephen Phillips from Amerenergy Incorporated in the studio and we'll ask him for some insight into this whole mess and what caused it."

The camera switches to Jim Stepe sitting in a chair adjacent to Stephen Phillips. "As Elaine said, I'm sitting here with Stephen Phillips of Amerenergy, the largest electric power generating company in the country. Welcome, Mr. Phillips. It's good of you to come down and talk with us."

"I'm glad I could have this opportunity to make clear some of the problems all of the generating companies are having trying to get power to the customers, where it's needed."

"How did you make it to our studio? Nothing is moving on the streets of New York as everyone could see from Tony's live report from Times Square."

"I came on one of Amerenergy's helicopters. We landed right on your helipad on the roof here."

"Where did you fly in from?"

"From our ship in New York harbor."

"I saw pictures of the ship. It's quite a ship isn't it?"

"Yes."

"I guess it's lucky that you have a ship in the harbor rather than a building downtown. Isn't it Mr. Phillips."

"Why do you say lucky?"

"I suspect that if you had a building here in Manhattan it would have been attacked by the angry mobs roving the streets."

"Why would they attack Amerenergy?"

"According to James Wilt of Contran, who was on our program while you were helicoptering over from your ship, Amerenergy is one of the major contributors to the blackout we're having."

"That's totally ridiculous."

"Mr. Wilt said that Amerenergy hasn't built any significant generating capacity in the past three years."

"There's been no need to."

"No need for more generating capacity?"

"No. You see Canada has plenty of capacity available in the summer when we need it because they're a winter peaking system. They use most of their electric power in the winter for heating, whereas we use most of our electricity in the summer for air conditioning."

Jim looks at his notes. "Mr. Wilt said that too, but he also said that a generating company can't just buy power from hundreds of miles away and expect to get it all to where it's needed because the transmission system wasn't designed to carry it."

"If the transmission system can't handle the load then the transmission companies should have built the transmission lines that could handle it."

Jim consults his notes again. "Mr. Wilt said it takes ten years and hundreds of millions of dollars to build the kind of transmission system that would be needed to bring all that power down from Canada to as far south as Georgia and South Carolina."

"Sure, and it would take ten years and billions of dollars to build the power generating plants right here in this country."

"So you think it's the transmission companies' fault that half the country is in total darkness tonight."

"I don't think it. I know it. There's plenty of generating capacity. The problem is there isn't enough transmission capacity. Look, it wasn't the generating plants that started melting down because there wasn't generating capacity, it was the transmission lines that melted down. The transmission system couldn't handle the loads so it's the transmission companies who are at fault."

"So it's not any of your responsibility?"

"Of course not. . . . As I said and will say again, it is purely a transmission problem."

"Did you offer to help pay for increasing the number of transmission lines?"

"No, transmission line investment is the responsibility of the transmission line companies."

"Before deregulation all the utilities built their own capacity in their own service areas didn't they."

"Not all of it. They purchased capacity from adjacent utilities."

"From adjacent utilities, but not adjacent countries."

"They purchased some from Canada."

Jim glances at his notes before continuing. "But not thirty or forty-percent of their total reserve capacity from Canada."

"I don't have the exact numbers."

"According to Mr. Wilt, Amerenergy has the lowest percentage of owned capacity reserves of any generating company in the country."

"Amerenergy has the highest profit margin of any generating company in the country. That shows that where deregulation is concerned we are doing the best job of getting the lowest cost power for our customers."

"Mr. Wilt said that Amerenergy shirked its responsibility to install adequate reserves near its customers' loads and that's what caused the meltdown of the mid-continent transmission system that ultimately brought down the whole eastern half of the country."

"Mr. Wilt is just trying to shift the blame away from where it belongs and that's on the transmission companies' doorsteps."

"All right. Let's change the subject just a bit. Now that we've had this catastrophic power failure. How do you think we should fix the system so it doesn't happen again?"

"That's simple. Build more and better transmission lines."

"Where?"

"In the mid-continent along north-south corridors."

"Mr. Wilt said that the transmission companies can't get the rightaways through all the states to get all the power you need from Canada."

"That's a problem that congress is going to have to deal with."

"Why congress?"

"Congress needs to make the laws that give the federal government the right to condemn land to build the transmission facilities needed. It's a national problem it requires a national solution."

"How come it wasn't a national problem before deregulation?"

"The power supply for the country was done differently when it was regulated."

"Deregulation has caused problems that no one could foresee?"

"No one tried deregulation here before, so no one knew for sure how it would work."

"So it was a big experiment?"

"It wasn't a big experiment. We knew it would work and it does work. We also knew it would take some minor adjustments along to way to make it work well."

"Minor adjustments, like we're having at the moment."

"This is just a temporary setback."

"We've had people shot down in Times Square because of this temporary setback."

"There are always a few who are hurt whenever there is a new technology or philosophy put in place. There are a few who are hurt if we don't put new technology in place."

"So a few people getting shot in the streets in New York is the price of progress?"

"Why are you trying to make Amerenergy out to be the bad guy here? Let's face it, Jim, New Yorkers get shot on your streets every day for breaking the law just like those teenagers did. Don't try to put their deaths on our backs or the transmission companies' backs."

"Mr. Phillips, who's going to pay for all the damages we've suffered here in the City?"

"What do you mean?"

"Five years ago the power went out in my neighborhood on Long Island and the power company that served us before Contran paid for all the loss of the food in my freezer. So who's going to pay for all the damages in the city?"

"Contran should pay the damages."

"Why Contran?"

"Contran is the one who connects the customers to the power system."

"But the generation companies supply the energy."

"Yes but it was the transmission system that failed."

"According to Mr. Wilt, it was the generating companies in general and Amerenergy in particular who caused the overload by not building the generating capacity where it's needed."

"We're going over old ground again, Jim. It was purely a transmission problem and if anyone should pay for the damages it should be the transmission companies."

"Will the transmission companies pay?"

"I doubt it. They will fight tooth and nail to avoid paying the damages. The total bill would bankrupt most if not all of the transmission companies in the eastern half of the country."

"Would it bankrupt Amerenergy?"

"It would if Amerenergy had to pay it, but believe me, it won't."

"Is that because Amerenergy has powerful friends in high places?"

"It won't because no court would find Amerenergy or any other energy company guilty of breaking any law."

"How about Contran?"

"The courts wouldn't find them guilty of breaking any laws either."

"How about negligence?"

"There's no case for negligence anywhere. We did our best and the transmission companies did their best under the system the government gave us."

"Isn't it the system you lobbied for?"

"Yes, but no one made congress deregulate the power system. It was their decision just like it was their decision to deregulate the airline, telephone, trucking and railroad industries."

"So it's the government's fault."

"Of course it the government's fault. There are hundreds of generating companies and hundreds of transmission companies but there's only one federal government who is responsible for the nation's power supply."

"Well I'm glad we finally discovered who's really responsible. I knew if we kept at it long enough the truth would come to the surface. Thank you, Mr. Phillips, for coming down and sharing your knowledge and viewpoint with us."

"I'm glad I could have the opportunity to clear up many of the contentious issues."

Jim turns to the camera, which comes in close. "You heard it here first. As it sometimes happens, Washington bears the ultimate responsibility for this national disgrace. Our congress seems to have put in motion an ill-thought-out plan that it wasn't sure would work. Or if they thought it would work, they didn't have any idea exactly how it would work. A federal experiment in progress that backfired and blacked out half the nation. It won't be rewarding for our senators or congressmen or congresswomen come next election, now will it? Back to you Elaine."

"Thank you, Jim for that enlightening interview. While we don't have many viewers at the moment due to the shortage of electrons flowing around the city at the moment, I'm sure our regular viewers will be eager to view a recording of that interview whenever the lights come back on." Elaine puts her hand over her left ear and listens. "I understand Tony Cochrane has made it across town to the United Nations where he will be interviewing Mr. Sumir Halibar, the UN representative from India. In recent years brownouts and rolling blackouts have become a way of life for the larger metropolitan areas of India. Mr. Halibar may be able to give us some insight or advice on how best to cope with an inadequate electric power system. You're live Tony."

Chapter 10

Audrey Calhoon is standing at the big board. The mayor of New York is at her side and Carlton Hayes is standing behind the mayor. Carlton asked Audrey to brief the mayor because he knows the mayor usually remains docile in the presence of an attractive woman.

All of the transmission lines are crosshatched in red. Audrey aims her laser pointer at the end of line twenty-six. "This is Boch Energy's Murtaugh oil-fueled steam plant." She moves the red laser dot down to the left about three feet. "And this is the Bentley Hydroelectric Project. We can't start the Murtaugh without enough electrical power to run the cooling water pumps, the fuel supply pumps, cooling tower fans and all the other auxiliary electrical equipment in the power station."

The mayor appears confused. "You can't start your electric generating plants to power the electrical system without first having electrical power in the system?"

"That's correct . . . for all generating plants except the hydroelectric units. They have enough batteries in their powerhouses to run their control equipment. Once we open the wicket gates on the hydro turbines they spin up to speed turning the generators and we have their full power. That's why they're so valuable in this kind of total blackout. We call it a black-start situation because there is no power at all in the system and all of the larger generating plants except the hydro units need a powered-up system to be able to be fired up, warmed up and slowly brought on line."

"This is a hell of a situation."

"You could say that. Since we've got no power and no way to electrically throw the switches, we've got to send out crews in trucks to each electrical switch we need to operate and have them physically throw the switch. We've got to isolate each steam plant then connect it to a hydroelectric plant or an adjacent operating area that's energized. Then we've got to bring each steam plant on line and bring its power up slowly without exceeding its thermal stress limitations. It can take up to several hours to bring each steam plant up to full power."

"And how many steam plants are we talking about?"

Audrey shifts her weight from one foot to the other, uneasily. "Well, our region has twelve steam electric plants including the Stronic Nuclear plant."

"And even the nuclear plant needs to be connected to an operating electrical system before it can be started?"

"That's right, Mayor. And once a plant is isolated from the loads and we get it up and running we can only connect a few distribution areas to the lines from the plant at a time because the plant has to be able to increase its power slowly. If we connect too much load to the plant at one time, it can't increase power quickly enough to provide enough power and the generator will slow down because the turbine can't provide enough horsepower and the frequency and voltage of the system drops and we can damage all kinds of our customers' equipment that's turned on. That's why it takes so long to bring up a system after a black start."

"How long will it take to get the city's power back on?"

"It's not just the city. The area we've got to bring up includes all of the boroughs, most of Long Island, parts of southern Connecticut and Eastern Jersey."

"How long?"

"We won't have it all back before late tomorrow afternoon and that's only if all goes well and we don't force a plant off after we get it part way up and have to bring it up from the bottom again."

The mayor looks over his shoulder at Carlton Hayes. "You've got to get the system back up before the sun goes down tomorrow night. The city will be totally devastated if it has to go through another night without lights and power. The damage estimate is already close to three-quarters of a billion. The city has lost one entire day of production. That's almost one quarter of one percent of the total annual productivity of the city. Do you have any idea how much the total productivity of the entire city of New York for one day is worth?"

Chapter 11

George has borrowed his neighbor's four-wheel-drive pickup truck and is driving across the Connecticut state line toward the Hastings' home. He's beginning to doubt that he will be able honor his promise to get some kind of backup power for Henry's respirator. He has stopped at every store he thought might possibly sell portable generators. There are none to be had anywhere.

His best hope is Watson's Hardware Store, which is only about seven miles from Henry's place. George was a frequent customer at Watson's before his and Liz's divorce. Watson's is only a small family-owned hardware store but it has always had everything George ever needed for his home projects. In his early years as a homeowner, whenever he couldn't find what he needed at the big chain hardware stores he tried Watson's as a last resort and never failed to find what he needed. He finally learned not to waste time at the large chain stores and in his last fifteen years as a homeowner shopped for his hardware needs exclusively at Watson's. Even if Watson's didn't have exactly what he needed, the old-timers who worked there could always come up with a way to jury-rig something that would work just as well. They were familiar with every item on every shelf at the store, unlike the dunderheads who worked at the large chain stores who didn't have a clue what was on any of the shelves anywhere in their stores.

George had to park in the street about a block away. Watson's parking lot was crammed full of homeowners trying desperately to find gadgets that would make life in the *big dark* a little easier. George pulled the store's front door open wide for a man coming out carrying a gas-fueled camping lantern, a camp stove, and a gallon can of lantern fuel.

The man looked stressed. "Thanks, I appreciate it. My arms are full."

"Maybe I should get one of those." George eyes the man's lantern.

"Too late, the guy right behind me got the last one."

"The story of my life," George said smiling and shaking his head.

"I know what you mean. I'm not usually this lucky."

George entered and scanned the faces in the store. John would be his best bet. He had always hit it off well with John. He had often gone out of his way to give George special help or attention. The inside of the store was lighted by three strategically located gas-fueled, double-sock camping lanterns suspended by wire from the steel roof trusses.

George spotted John in the back of the store. As he approached, George saw that John was hauling gallon cans of lantern fuel into the back door from the stockroom. There were at least twenty men and women waiting for the cans.

John announced, "There are only about fifteen gallons left. You all know the order you came in so be fair and don't take a can before your turn."

George was surprised that the customers were so cordial and orderly. There were no short tempers. The last of the cans of fuel was handed out and John raised the palms of his hands and shrugged his shoulders. "That's all she wrote, folks."

The remaining customers turned and ambled away without comment.

"Sorry George there's just no more."

"I didn't come for lantern fuel, John. I need to talk to you about a serious situation I have."

"Lets go into the storeroom. We can talk while I unload what's left of our stock of batteries."

George followed John and noted the stockroom was lit with one battery-powered electric lantern. "I'll help."

"You don't need to do that. You're almost a charter customer."

"I need to do it for my own peace of mind."

"Suit yourself." John points to a palate, about three feet square, loaded with shrink-wrapped battery packs of all shapes and sizes.

"What a load of batteries. Looks like you were expecting this run on batteries."

"We were. Old man Watson has been saying for months this deregulation was headed for a derailment. He ordered this palate of batteries two months ago."

"I bet you could sell them for a pretty penny."

"I'm sure we could but that's not the way we do business at Watson's. We'll do fine anyway because old man Watson got a special discount . . . it was an unusually large order."

"What should I do with them?"

"Let's just put them in the shopping cart behind you and we'll roll it out the front to restock the battery rack."

John pulls a penknife from his pocket, opens it, and cuts through the triple layer of plastic wrap surrounding the whole mass of battery packs. "What is it you want to talk about?"

"I have a friend who lives about six miles up the road. He has lung problems and is on a respirator. The respirator's backup batteries have about four hours left in them."

"That's not good. This thing isn't going to be over in four hours. Hell, it might not be over for a couple of days."

"Yeah, I know. I need a portable generator or I'm afraid Henry won't make it."

John wrinkles his brow and purses his lips. He remains quite for almost a minute, deep in thought. He shakes his head. "That's a bummer. There aren't any generators to be had anywhere. We had two we used for our own backup but old man Watson sent them over to the Sunup Nursing Home. They have four residents on some kind of life-support."

"You were my last hope. I have no ideas left. The unit runs on backup batteries but I've checked everywhere and there aren't any to be had. Even if there were some available, they come from the factory discharged."

"How does the unit work?" John was intrigued.

"It has an electric motor that runs off hundred-and-ten-volt AC power."

"What about the batteries? They're not AC."

"No. It has a converter to change the forty-eight-volt battery power to AC and then a transformer to kick it up to one-ten volts."

"So the only option is one-ten-volt AC power?"

"That's right, a portable one-ten volt AC generator."

"No, you're being too restrictive, think out of the box. Just one-ten volts AC—who cares if it comes from a portable generator?"

"You're right. Forget portable generator, just one hundred and ten volts of alternating current."

"That's right. Now think. How can we get one-ten AC current?"

"A wall plug . . . all I can think of is a damn wall plug." George slams his fist down on the battery palate.

"Come on, George, that's not out-of-the-box thinking."

"I know but lately I've been a stuck-in-the-box kind of thinker."

"You know what that's from?"

"What?"

"All that beer you've been putting away."

"What are you talking about?"

"Come on, George. You know Milly works at the ConnWay grocery where you buy your two cases a week."

"Oh. You've been spying on me."

"Milly's just been a mite worried about you is all."

"John, let's get back to the problem at hand—one-ten-volts AC."

"Yeah, you know I worked for Hepples and McRory before I retired and came to Watson's."

"What's Hepples and McWhatever's?"

"McRory . . . it's an engineering consulting firm. We did a lot of corrosion consulting work back in the seventies."

"And your point is?"

"We needed one-ten-volt power to run our test equipment when we were in the field."

"And?"

"The mechanics at the motor pool wired into the alternators on our trucks and put regular outlets right under our dash so we could plug in our equipment."

"You got one-ten volts AC from your truck alternators?"

"Yeah."

"Do you think we could do it?"

"Don't see why not. We'll just pull your alternator, open it up, run some number twelve electrical wire through the vents on the back, solder the wires to the two poles of the alternator where they're soldered to the three diodes which convert the AC to DC and we get AC power."

"You make it sound simple."

"It's straightforward surgery and we've got all the surgical instruments we need right here."

Chapter 12

Maria is exhausted. She's functioning on nothing but adrenalin. Carlos is a nervous wreck. He's caught in a pitch-black hell with Maria, a forever limbo, fluctuating between contractions and short spells of relief. Three hours of Maria's painful contractions have convinced him that the baby will be forever encased in her pelvis. The air in the elevator is stale and wet. Maria and Carlos are both slippery with sweat.

The two are totally dependent on each other's touch. When Carlos isn't touching her, Maria feels disoriented, as if she falling through a black vacuum. Carlos can only relate to the situation when he can feel his wife's sweat-slippery hips, thighs and distended groin. He can feel his son's wrinkled and hairy scalp ringed by the edges of Maria's tightly stretched vagina.

Dean Collins calls up from below. His voice is very faint. "I couldn't get through on the telephone. I called nine-one-one but could only get a busy signal. I went outside and found a cop. I told him about you and he said he would relay a message to the fire department."

Carlos shouts back, "Did he say how long?"

"What?"

Carlos shouts more loudly. "Did he say how long?"

"No. He said the fire department is really busy."

"Can you get something and pry open the elevator doors?"

Dean thinks a moment."I have a lug wrench in the trunk of my car. That might do it."

Chapter 13

The subway tunnel is totally dark. For the passengers, their only useful senses are their touch and hearing. They are standing on some kind of narrow ledge or walkway, shuffling their feet in small side steps. They are facing the concrete wall of the tunnel and feeling it with their fingertips as they move. There are many voices in the darkness. Some voices are very close and others are in the far distance.

A woman's voice asks, "How do we know which way to go?"

A man answers, "We don't, but what does it matter? There will be a station no matter which way we go."

"Yeah, but one way might be only a little ways and the other may be blocks and blocks."

"Just keep moving. We'll get to a station sometime."

"How will we know when we get to one?"

"We'll feel the platform. The tunnel wall will end and there will be a platform."

"I'd hate to miss the station the dark and go right past it."

"Don't worry so much. That can't happen. Besides, there will probably be some kind of emergency battery lights, won't there?"

"How long do battery lights last? We've been down here for hours now."

"You're a born pessimist."

There is a woman's scream in the distance.

"What was that?" a woman asks.

"I don't know." A man yells, "What happened?"

"Someone stepped off the walkway and fell down onto the tracks." It's a distant voice.

There is a woman's wail in the distance. "I broke my arm. I broke my arm!"

"I'll come down and help you. Keep talking so I don't climb down on you."

"It hurts. It hurts so bad!"

"You'll be okay. Just don't touch the steel rails. If the power comes back on you could get electrocuted."

"It won't be okay. I feel the bone sticking out. My arm is wet. I'm bleeding, I'm bleeding." The woman wails.

A man's voice from further away shouts, "Where's the woman with the gun? Hey, woman with the gun, shoot the bitch with the broken arm and put her out of her misery."

"You're an asshole," comes another man's voice.

The voices of the injured woman, her helper, and her tormentor grow more faint as the leaders of the expedition move further along the cool, damp tunnel wall.

Chapter 14

The cabby had been right. When Martin Walters finally reached Wall Street, the market was closed tighter than a boxer's fist in the first round of a bout. It is dark on the streets because there is a new moon. He has been walking for almost two hours and is still six blocks from his hotel. He feels totally vulnerable because the streets are owned by hoodlums.

Martin's shoe soles crackle on the broken glass from the plate glass windows which have been smashed along his route. The only light he can navigate by comes from the occasional burning hulk of a car. The flickering firelight gives New York's streets the eerie look of a si-fi movie. The young men, out and about, are bent on destruction.

At one intersection Martin sneaks past the corner of a building. He can see the curb by the dim light of a burning car at the far end of the block. He walks quickly toward the street, with its tangled mass of abandoned vehicles. He hears a shout.

"There's a guy at the other end of the block. Let's get him."

Martin starts to run. The cars in the street are so tightly packed together that he can't move quickly between them and jumps from hoods to trunks. To his right he can hear the sound of feet running on the sidewalk and feet clambering across automobile sheet steel. Some are trying to catch him while others are trying to cut him off. He finally realizes the futility of his flight and jumps down between two cars. He duck-walks about fifty feet and then lays flat on the pavement. His predators are getting closer. He works himself under a Checker cab which has good ground clearance. He lies perfectly still and forces himself to breathe slowly so the sound of his breathing won't expose his location.

"Where is he?"

"I don't know. I heard him last running across the cars somewhere near here."

"He must be hiding between the cars, or, maybe under one."

"We need some light."

"I'll give us some light."

Martin hears something metal hitting a steel container repeatedly, followed by the sound of liquid splashing onto the pavement.

"Who's got a match?"

Martin realizes with panic that it was the sound of a knife hitting the bottom of a gas tank. He hears the faint sound of a match striking a matchbook, followed by the *woomph* of an explosion of flammable fumes. Suddenly, he can see all too well. He can see the feet of his tormentors only four cars away.

"Look under the cars," a voice orders.

In the bright flickering light, Martin sees faces peering at him from under cars only forty feet away. His heart sinks, he's cornered—trapped, screwed, blued and tattooed. The feet are coming quickly toward him and he moves further under the car, trying his best to find a location equidistant from the sides of the Checker cab and the feet surrounding his not-so-concealed hiding place.

"Come out or we'll drag you out."

After a moment of silence, "Okay, grab him and pull him out."

Martin feels a hand close on his right ankle. He tries to expand in the narrow space to resist the pull. The pull increases and he is dragged about a foot. His head is forced down by the car's muffler, and his front tooth jambs into the asphalt and chips. He is stunned by the pain, stops resisting, and is dragged quickly from under the cab.

Johnny Capello is with the mob of hoodlums but his heart isn't. He has a difficult time identifying his friends in their present state of mind. They have always been a bit wild but they are totally out of control and he feels sick to his stomach. He can't help visualizing the disappointment and disapproval in his mother's face for everything he has done since darkness fell. His compatriots have grown in boldness as the darkness has grown and now they can only be considered animal predators. He doesn't even recognize Juan as the best friend he has known for nine years.

He watches in stunned silence as they stomp the nicely dressed man. He is unconscious but they continue to kick at him, as if his continuing to breathe is an insult. The batteries in Johnny's flashlight had burned out at least an hour earlier and Juan now carries the flashlight as a weapon. He clubs Martin on the back of the head twice with it. To break the frenzied attack, Johnny shouts, "Get his wallet and watch." The diversion works. The young men roll Martin over and go though his pockets.

"Got them," shouts a shorthaired young man in a dirty T-shirt. The group instinctively surveys the empty street to see if anyone witnessed their actions.

"Let's go," Juan shouts.

The group works it way out of the tight knot of cars to the sidewalk but Johnny falls behind. He hides between a sport utility vehicle and a wrecker. The mass of young men moves up the street looking for prey.

When they are out of sight, Johnny works his way back to where the nicely dressed man lays crumpled between the vehicles. Johnny leans down close to the man's face and hears a faint wheezy breath. Several cars are now engulfed in flames and the area is well lighted. The man looks to be in his thirties and his profile is much like his uncle Jim's. Johnny starts whimpering at the thought that his uncle could easily be in a similar condition somewhere across town.

After an hour or so, the flames are almost out, and the man moans.

"Are you okay?" Johnny asks, knowing only too well the answer.

"Uh, I'm sick." Martin rolls to his side and vomits violently. He vomits repeatedly, but nothing comes up. He falls into unconsciousness again.

Fifteen minutes pass and Martin moans again. He rolls onto his back.

"Just lie still," Johnny says in a soothing voice.

"What happened," Martin's mind is a total blank.

"You were beaten up. You're in pretty bad shape."

"I was in a fight?"

"No. You were just beat up. You didn't fight back."

"Who are you?"

"I'm Johnny Capello. Who are you?"

"I'm Martin Walters."

"What do you do, Mr. Walters?"

"What do you mean?"

"What kind of work do you do?"

"I don't know. I feel sick."

"You have been throwing up."

"My head hurts so badly." Martin turns to his side again and vomits violently before falling back into unconsciousness.

It's only about five minutes before Martin stirs again. He asks, "What happened?"

"I told you. You were beaten."

"I was in a fight?"

"No. You were just beaten. You asked me that just a few minutes ago don't you remember?"

"No. I don't remember anything. My head hurts and I feel sick to my stomach. Who are you?"

"I'm Johnny Capello. I told you that just a few minutes ago. Don't you remember?"

"No. I feel sick. I think I have to puke."

"I don't doubt it."

Chapter 15

Elaine is looking haggard. The active, engaging tone is gone from her voice. She is reading the news as one would read a label on a soup can in a grocery store isle.

"This morning the sun rises on a still darkened city. Contran says that they're having trouble getting enough power from the generating companies to get the system back up because too many customers still have too many of their appliances turned on. Contran says that every time a generating company starts a plant and connects it to the system it has too much load to serve and it slows down and has to be taken off line to keep from burning the generators up.

Come on New York. Get with the program. If you all don't go through your houses and turn off and unplug all your major appliances we'll never get the system up and running again. If you can hear this broadcast, go tell your neighbors to turn everything off. If you can't hear this broadcast then to hell with you."

The director in the studio orders the broadcast switched to a live feed with Tony Cochrane standing in front of a large power plant cooling tower.

Tony is leaning against a chain link fence half asleep. He suddenly comes alive and blinks at the camera. "Uh, this is Tony Chochrane coming to you live from the Chitahook steam electric generating plant in southwestern Connecticut."

That white monster behind me is the cooling tower which cools the used steam after it goes through the generators and turns it back into water to be fed back to the boilers. Normally it's spewing clouds of steam. As you can see, it's not doing much of anything right now.

I tried to get an interview with the plant supervisor but he declined. He said he was too busy at the moment but busy doing what is what I, and I'm sure you all, want to know. It seems to me that it's long past time to get this plant and the others in the region started.

There is talk in Washington that this whole blackout is nothing more than a ploy by the generating companies to get the price caps lifted so they can pocket some really big profits. There are committee meetings in progress on Capitol Hill at which there are murmurings by some senators and some representatives to scrap the whole idea of deregulation and go back to a regulated industry.

The experts we've talked to, say almost unanimously that it would be almost impossible to get our old system back. The consensus is that once the utilities were broken up and sold the fate of deregulation was sealed. Almost to a man, they say the power industry is much like Humpty Dumpty and all the king's horses and all the king's men wouldn't be able to put it back together and regulate it again, even if they wanted to.

Those same experts say the best we can do is to put controls and minimum requirements in place that will allow the industry to grow without putting the general population and the public interest and national security at risk. It's obvious that the deregulated power industry, as it presently exists, has become a threat to everyone's security, safety, and well being.

This is Tony Chochrane signing off for the moment at the Chitahook steam electric generating plant. I hope you have a better day today than the night you had last night."

Chapter 16

Audrey Calhoon is studying a large map spread out on the floor of the control room. Paul Dabson is sitting on the floor beside her. The other controllers are working feverishly at their consoles.

Carlton Hayes is nowhere to be seen. His absence makes Audrey's job easier and less stressful but it also makes her a bit uncomfortable. She knows that he's likely trying to distance himself from the activity so that if the situation gets worse, which is probable, he can claim negligence on the part of his subordinates. She is confident that his attempts to protect himself will be in vain. No one at Contran will be able to shield themselves from the fallout that's sure to follow. Contran is the last variable in the power equation and will be the logical choice when anyone goes looking for a scapegoat.

Audrey picks up the two-way radio and presses the transmit button. "Three-seven, this is control. Come in please."

"Three-seven here," the supervisor of crew thirty-seven answers.

"You are going to have to pull the breakers on lines fifty-six and fifty-eight at Brackston and on twenty-six and thirty-five at Cornelis to isolate the Watkins-Hawk sub area. They are back-feeding the two-fifty-kV line through the transformers connected to the sixty-nine-kV buss at the Watkins substation and that's why we can't get isolation."

"Which lines are those again?"

"Write this down. Lines fifty-six and fifty-eight at Brackston and twenty-six and thirty-five at Cornelis."

"Okay. I got it."

"How long thirty-seven?"

"Fifteen minutes for Brackston and another forty-five for Cornelis."

"Can't you make it faster? We don't have an hour to lose."

"Sorry, Control. An hour is what it will take . . . minimum."

"Roger that, thirty-seven. Give me a call when it's done so I can notify Amerenergy to start their Hawk combined-cycle units. Out"

"Roger that, Control. Out."

Paul Dabson asks, "What are you going to do after Hawk is back on line?"

"We need to cut all the subs from the Hawk-Swank line so we can get all of Hawk's power to Swank steam plant. Once we have Swank back on line we'll have enough power to supply the whole Stephens sub-area and get the Stephens steam plant on line." Audrey runs her right hand though her hair. It's the only concern she has shown for her personal appearance in forty-eight hours.

"That's good. I think if we can get Hawk and Swank both on line at the same time we can get back the whole southeastern quadrant." Paul draws an imaginary circle around the Hawk and Swank plants with the tip of his finger.

"Yeah, but only if we can get the crews to make sure that no more customers than we can serve are connected to the system."

"That's the problem. None of the scenarios we ran in our simulations are anywhere close to what's happening out there in the real world. The computer experts are going to have to go back to the drawing board. Their black-start procedure is not working as it was supposed to."

Chapter 17

George Tower drives away from the alley behind the hardware store and John waves. "Good luck."

George shouts from his open window, "Thanks. If this works, you're a genius . . . and a saint. Hell, you're a saint even if it doesn't work. You can be the patron saint of *the whole nine yards.*"

George looks down at the truck's dash and swears, "shit, low on gas."
He drives toward Henry's place and examines every gas station along the highway. They all have *out of service* signs posted.

Several miles farther on, George approaches a gas station that captures his attention. This gas station is different from all the others in that a man is sitting out by the pumps in a rocking chair. The man looks to be in his sixties, with snow-white hair ringing the bald spot on the top of his head.

George pulls into the station and stops twenty feet short of the chair. He climbs out and ambles toward the man. "Afternoon. You don't happen to be open do you?"

The man points a finger at the sign on the large garage door. *Closed for the duration.*

"I'm in a real bind. I have a friend on a respirator who's going to die if I don't get this truck over to his house and I'm low on gas."

"Can't help you there. I can sell you cans of oil and gallons of antifreeze or any number of candy bars, but not a drop of gas."

"Pumps don't work?"

"Not well without electricity."

"You don't have a portable generator to run the pumps do you?"

"I'd be selling millions of gallons of gasoline . . . I'd probably be totally out of gas by now if I had a portable generator to run my pumps."

"Can I buy some gas if I can figure a way to get in from your tanks into my truck?"

"Sure, if you can do it without blowing up the place. But there's no way. I've thought about it a lot."

"Yeah, but I bet you've been thinking inside the box." George said it with a smirk.

"What's that mean?" The old man thinks George is making fun of him.

"John over at Watkin's Hardware store showed me how to think out of the box. You think you can't pump gas because you aren't breaking the problem down into its most basic components. Why can't you pump gas?"

"I can't pump gas because there's no electricity to run the pumps."

"There's no electricity coming from the electric service in your station, but is that the only way to pump gas? Do you have any kind of mechanical pump?"

"No. The only pumps in the place are the small pumps that go in the gas tanks of the cars we work on. The fuel pump pushes gas up to the carburetor or fuel injection system but they're all just little pumps that work on twelve-volt battery power."

"Now you're talking. See what happens when you think out of the box?"

"You think we can pump gas out of my underground tanks with a twelve-volt in-tank fuel pump?"

"Sure, why not?"

"The pump would have to be submerged and the gas level in the tanks is about four feet below ground."

"You have electrical wire, don't you?"

"Sure." The old man looks skeptical.

"You have rolls of fuel line, I bet."

"Yeah, but putting a fuel pump down into an underground tank with long electrical wires and a long quarter-inch fuel line sounds a mite dangerous."

"The fuel pumps run inside the gas tanks of cars don't they?"

"Yeah, but it seems to be stretching things to run one inside a large underground tank."

"I think it'll work."

"It might, but it will take a bit of work and a lot of time."

"You look like you have a bit of time to spare and I can do the work."

"What do I get out of it?"

"You get to save a good man's life, what more do you want out of it. I'll give you a hundred bucks for a fill-up."

"Nah. You're right, saving a man's life is more than enough . . . at least it should be. I'll charge you for the wire and the fuel line and fifteen bucks for the gas."

"What about the cost of the fuel pump? They're a bit expensive . . . several hundred bucks I've heard."

"That's true but they last for many years and after we're done with it, I'll still be able to sell it. No one will know the difference."

"You are a good man Charlie Brown but I detect a bit of larceny in you."

"A bit of larceny in an old man makes him exciting to the ladies."

"I bet you have to beat them off with a stick."

"Used to when I was a mite younger but now the ladies I see are a bit older with fragile skin. Sticks will bring out the age spots."

The old man pulled on the chain that raised the garage door and the two went to work in bay number one. It took less than a half hour to rig a Chevrolet fuel pump with thirty feet of quarter-inch fuel line and two forty-foot electric wires — a red one to the hot connection of the pump motor and a black one to the ground connection.

"Okay let's try this baby out." The old man has become an eager participant in the out-of-the-box experiment. "Pull your truck over there by the filler connection." He points to a white-painted, nine-inch steel cover sunk into the concrete apron in front of the garage doors.

The old man lifted the small steel cover with a screwdriver blade. He removed the six-inch snap cover from the tank filler pipe and slowly lowered the pump down into the tank with the wires and rubber fuel line.

George parks beside the filler pipe and opens the truck's hood. Then the old man secures the black wire to the battery's negative, or ground, terminal and the red wire to the positive battery terminal with two large clips he took off an old set of jumper cables. The pump starts immediately and gasoline squirts out of the end of the fuel line onto the concrete.

"Whoa, I wasn't ready for that quite yet." The old man jumps back, surprised that the system works at all. He quickly disconnects the leads from the truck's battery. "Put the fuel line into the truck's filler and I'll hook it up again."

George removes the gas cap and sticks the quarter-inch rubber line into the filler neck. "It'll probably take quite a while to fill it up."

"Maybe so but at least it'll work. Nothing else does."

"Do you have any gas cans? I probably should take a couple of filled cans just to be sure."

"I've got some one-gallon gas cans for sale inside but you don't want them. Go out back and in the small store room with the green door you'll find three five-gallon Jerry cans. You can borrow them."

"Thanks, I really appreciate it."

It was twenty minutes before the truck's filler neck began to overflow and another ten before the three Jerry cans were full.

"Thanks," George says to the old man, handing him a fifty-dollar bill.

"Too much. It's thirty at most."

"Take it. You deserve all of it and more. Don't make me feel bad."

"Okay, but just so you won't feel bad."

George climbs into the truck and starts the engine, throws the truck in gear, and starts to pull away. He yells out the window. "You're a gentleman and a scholar."

The old man shouts at the truck as it pulls away. "I'm just an ornery old codger and don't you forget it."

"You're a saint." George shouts with his head out his window as he pulls out of the driveway onto the deserted highway.

Twenty minutes later, George turns into the driveway of 2315 Euclid Street. He turns the truck off the concrete drive onto the grass and pulls the pickup to a stop close to the front door of Henry and Emma Lou Hastings' home. He climbs out of the truck and pulls the extra-heavy-duty extension cord from the bed of the truck. He plugs the male end of the cord into the upper outlet of the dual-plug outlet he and John, the hardware guru, mounted on the dash, and unrolls the extension cord to the front door.

Emma Lou had heard George's truck come up the drive and opens the front door. "Thank God you're here. You're George?"

"That's me, Mrs. Hastings. How's Henry?"

"He's okay for the moment but the batteries must be very low in the respirator because it's slowing down."

"Well, I have some one-ten power here in the truck." He hurries back to the pickup as he speaks, "I'll just have to make sure the engine's running fast enough to put out the one-ten volts we need." He jumps back in the truck and plugs the leads of a volt meter that John had given him into the lower receptacle of the outlet. The needle on the voltmeter swings to ninety-two volts. He takes the short length of two-by-four board that John had cut for him and braces it between the truck's accelerator pedal and the front of the driver's seat. The truck's engine idle speed picks up. The volt meter jumps to one-hundred-three volts. George fiddles with the two-by-four and the gage finally reads one-hundred-twelve volts. "Good enough for government work."

George rushes back to the front door. He picks up the roll of extension cord and rolls line off as he quickly follows Emma Lou to her Husband's bed in the back bedroom.

"Well if it isn't George, the Saint, Tower." Henry's face is a pasty color and his smiling lips are a blue-grey.

"Just call me Ready Milliwatt," George says with a wink. He pulls the respirator's plug from the dead wall outlet and plugs it into the female end of the extension cord. The respirator immediately increases speed as the indicator light switches from *Battery Power* to *External Power*.

"Oh, thank the Lord." Emma Lou puts her hands to her mouth and tears of joy fill her age-greyed eyes.

Chapter 18

"Where are you? Shout so I can tell if you're on a floor above me or below me." Carlos hears the man's shout and calls out, "We're here. We're here."

"You're above me. I'll go up to the next floor."

After a few moments silence Carlos hears, "Where are you?"

"We're here," Carlos shouts.

"You're still above me. I'll go up another floor."

Another silence followed by "Where are you?"

"We're here."

"Now you're below me. You must be between floors nine and ten. I'll try prying open the outer doors here."

"Okay," Carlos shouts back.

Carlos hears the sound of the steel tire iron prying between the doors then the man's faint voice, "I got the outer doors partially open, but the elevator is too far down. I'm going down to the next floor and try there."

Maria screams out in pain. She's having another contraction. Carlos is worried. The doctor said that Maria has a very small pelvis and that she might not be able to deliver the baby. The doctor said that he may have to give her a caesarean section if she can't deliver vaginally. Carlos hears the steel tire iron prying the doors again but this time the sound is below him.

The voice is louder, "I got the outer doors open. Now I'm going to try to get the inner doors apart."

Carlos shouts, "Please hurry!" He can see a faint light in the narrow slit between the doors.

The doors open about a foot and Carlos sees the outline of the man's face just about a foot above the floor. There is a candle burning on the hallway floor behind the man.

"Help me," the man groans, as he tries to force the doors open more.

Carlos stands and, facing the doors, pulls them apart with all his strength. The doors open all of a sudden and Carlos has to catch himself from falling out into the hallway. "Gracias . . . gracias!" he gasps.

"How is your wife?"

"She's not good. She's in much pain."

"I'm a medical student. I know about childbirth but I've never delivered a baby."

"The doctor said Maria may be too small to deliver the baby. He said she might have to have a caesarian operation."

"That's not good. We have to get her to the hospital right away."

Maria cries out in pain again.

In the dim candle light, Carlos cannot see the concern on the young man's face. "Can we move her?"

"We've got to move her to get her to the hospital. As soon as her contraction passes you've got to pull her over to the doors."

"How will we get her out? She can't walk."

"I'll pull her out and let her down easily to the floor. How big is she?"

"She's really big with the baby."

"I mean how much does she weigh?"

"She weighed about one ten before the baby. Now maybe one forty."

"She's small. We should have no trouble with her."

Maria relaxes as the contraction passes. "It's not bad now. What is your name, senior?"

"I'm Dean Connors. What's your name?"

"I'm Maria and this is my husband, Carlos."

Carlos moves around to her head and grabs her under the arm pits. He pulls her around so his back is to the door and drags her until he feels Dean's hand on the back of his knee. "That's far enough. Now if she can just schooch back until her head and shoulders are out over the edge, I can grab her."

Maria pushes with her hands and wiggles toward the opening and the hallway. Dean pushes his hands under her shoulders and grabs her under the arm pits as Carlos had. He pulls and she lets out a squeal in panic.

"It'll be okay," he assures her.

"I'll fall!" Maria shouts. She's as stiff as a board.

"I've got you. I won't let you fall." He drags her out of the elevator and when her heels clear the edge, Dean trips on his own feet and falls back. Maria falls on him. Maria thinks that he makes a great cushion.

"Oh, gracias senior." Maria weeps with relief as Dean gasps to catch his breath. Maria's fall had knocked the wind out of him.

It's only a moment before Dean is on his feet again beside the doors. "Jump down," he implores.

Carlos jumps down to the hallway floor but misjudges the distance. He lands off balance and staggers backwards toward the gaping hole below the elevator's floor. He will continue to backpedal into the abyss if Dean doesn't stop him.

Standing beside the open doors, Dean sticks out his right arm and catches Carlos across the shoulders. He puts all is weight against Carlos' back and stops Carlos' fall. His action throws him off balance and directly into the abyss. "Oh shit!" are the last words out of his mouth.

Carlos hears the young man hit the far wall then a few seconds later impact in the basement.

"Oh, Mi Dios!" Carlos shouts. Then he and Maria weep as Maria enters yet another contraction.

Chapter 19

In the subway tunnel, the long line of men and women shuffle along the walkway in the darkness at a snail's pace, their noses almost touching the damp concrete tunnel wall.

A voice calls out. "I see a faint light."

"I see it too," comes a rapid reply.

The long line of frightened humans finally sees the proverbial light at the end of the tunnel, not figuratively but actually. The snail's pace increases to a fast side step. It is only five minutes more before the first man in line reaches the subway station. He climbs quickly onto the platform and gives the man behind a helping hand. The only light is filtering down the winding stairway at the far end of the station.

Two men, who have been helping their loudmouthed gunshot buddy, boost the wounded man onto the platform, where he rolls over onto his back and lets out a moan. In the faint light, they can see he is soaked from the waist down in his own blood.

One man, climbing on the platform beside the wounded man, shakes his head. "We'd better get a cab or call an ambulance and get him to a hospital. He must be in shock."

The other man climbs up on the platform. "I'm sure he's in shock. Hell, he keeps passing out."

The two men lift their bloody buddy and, supporting him under his shoulders between them, stagger to the subway station stairs. After struggling up the long stairway, the two are shocked when they come out into the bright sunlight. There are no cabs to hail and traffic is at a standstill. When they examine the cars in the street more carefully, they realize that all of the cars have been abandoned. The only traffic moving is foot traffic on the sidewalks. Several pedestrians slow to stare at the two men and their bloody cargo.

"What the hell are you looking at?" One shouts at the curious onlookers. "Where's the nearest hospital?"

A shrunken old woman points a claw of a finger up the street. "'Elmhurst, 'bout ten blocks."

"Thanks," one of the two shouts.

The two men fall into an uneven and broken cadence as the toes of their buddy's shoes drag the sidewalk behind them. The one who thanked the old lady mutters, "The old bag probably is armed."

The other quickly adds, "Yeah, but at least she's too old to suffer from PMS."

Chapter 20

Johnny Capello supports Martin Walters and helps him up the sidewalk. Johnny is sure the man will die if he doesn't get him some medical attention. No one can puke and fall unconscious as much as this man without dying in the end. He figures the man's brains must be like jelly from the beating he took.

"Where are we?" Martin asks.

"We're headed to the hospital."

"What's a hospital?"

"A hospital is where they will make you better."

"Who are you?"

"I'm Johnny Capello. Who are you?"

"I'm Martin Walters."

"What do you do for a living?"

"A living? What's that? Oh, I feel sick."

"Do you want to stop and puke?"

"Yes let me puke. I'm sick." Martin falls to his knees for the eighth time in thirty-five minutes. His knees are bloody but he doesn't notice. He vomits nothing but small bursts of air from his sore and swollen throat.

Chapter 21

Elaine speaks at the camera. There is no conviction in her words. "We've gotten a report from Contran that it's taking longer than expected to get the system back up and running. That's what we call an understatement. It's going on twenty-six hours now and New York is a shamble. All of the roads are nothing more than parking lots, everyone is exhausted, food is spoiling without refrigeration, only those with gas stoves can cook anything, the water pressure is dropping to minimum levels because the city's water purification system is out of service and the pumps that keep the water pressures up are all electric and out of service. If we all don't die of hunger we'll surely fall victim to thirst and dehydration. In my little earphone, I hear my producer telling me to keep the message upbeat. Well, there's nothing to be upbeat about. The system is failing and there seems to be no end to the numbers of disasters that can befall this great city of ours."

The few TV sets that are still working in the city go blank for a moment. When their pictures return, Elaine is gone, replaced by a fresh young man.

"I'm Todd Lindsay, sitting in for Elaine Mercer here at Channel Seven News. Elaine is exhausted as everyone should expect after being on the air for more than a full day. Elaine will be back after she gets a few winks of shuteye. In the meantime, be assured that Contran is doing all it can do to get the power system up and running again. They assure us that it will be only several hours more."

Chapter 22

George wakes up and stretches. He glances around and realizes he's on the Hastings' front porch swing. He's been asleep since about midnight. He glances at his watch. It's seven-thirty-seven. He gets up and quickly goes to the truck. He sticks his head into the window and reads the gas gage. "Oh, shit, only an eighth of a tank." He runs back to the front door, pulls the screen door open and rushes in.

Emma Lou hears George come in and comes quickly from the back bedroom. "You seem upset. What is it?"

"I used up all the gas in the gas cans and the truck is down to only an eighth of a tank. We have to get Henry and his respirator to the Sisters of Mercy Hospital where they have more reliable electric power."

"This is working fine."

"It is now but the truck's gas is running out and none of the gas stations' pumps work so we can't get more."

"How can we get Henry to the hospital?"

"We'll leave him hooked up to the respirator and we'll put him and the machine in the bed of the pickup, still connected to the truck's one-ten power."

"That'll work?"

"Don't see why it wouldn't. The hospital's only eight miles so we should make it with gas to spare. Does Henry have a wheelchair?"

"Yes, it's in the other bedroom just down the hall."

"I'll get it. Do you think your neighbors will help move the respirator?"

"Of course, they're all good people."

The lights in the house come on dimly then brighten slowly to full brilliance. Henry stares dumbly at the lamp on the night stand beside his bed. "I'll be damned. We made it."

Emma Lou sits down in the chair beside the bed. She relaxes and the air rushes out of her lungs in a sigh of ultimate relief.

After a few minutes, George unplugs the respirator from the end of the extension cord and plugs it into the wall socket beside Emma Lou's chair. As he does so, the respirator switches momentarily to *Battery Power* and then back to *External Power*.

"That's more like it." George is greatly relieved. A tremendous load falls from his shoulders.

"Why didn't we take Henry to the Sisters of Mercy Hospital right away if they have a reliable electric system? Why did you rig this system from the truck?"

"The hospital didn't have a reliable power supply until last night. It had only a battery backup system that was good for only about eight hours. We'd have been no better off waiting for the hospital's batteries to run down than we were waiting for the respirator's batteries to run down. I heard on the radio that the national guard would be moving in two of their big diesel units last night and would have them up and running this morning."

Chapter 23

Carlton Hayes paces the glassed-in booth overlooking the operations floor. He bites his nails nervously. Joshua Hunt, Contran's general manager, is standing just inside the door of the booth watching Carlton and the action on the floor. On the floor, Audrey Calhoon is on the telephone. She speaks a few words and then listens for almost thirty seconds. She finally puts the telephone down and stands up.

"We're in trouble people!" She shouts. "That was PennYork Gas on the phone. It seems that they're losing pressure in the Erie interstate gas supply line. The main pumping station just outside of Erie is powered by electricity and, without power the pumps, it won't keep the gas pressure up. The only gas they can deliver is that which is already in the line and pressurized. The line normally runs at a pressure of over two-thousand pounds per square inch but is now down to five-hundred. If the pressure falls below three hundred, the natural-gas fueled electric generating plants in the entire region will shut down or won't come on line if they are already down. That's 15 percent of our total generating capacity. If that happens, the plants we already have on line will be overloaded and trip off again. We've got to find a way to get power to the Erie gas pumping station or we may be totally out of business for who knows how long. We can't let that happen. We need to cut some areas off that are currently powered up and get some circuits open to Erie. That's not a request, that's an order."

Carlton picks up a microphone and announces to everyone on the floor. "This is Carlton Hayes. Belay that order. Don't shut down anyone that currently has power. We don't know what they're doing with that power and can't take any chances that we'll cut someone off that has a critical need."

The general manager rips the microphone from Carlton's hand and brings it up to his mouth. He depresses the key. "This is Joshua Hunt, general manager. You're to ignore that last order by Mr. Hayes. Mr. Hayes no longer has any authority in operations matters. Until further notice, you are to take orders from Miz. Calhoon on the operations floor. You all are doing a great job. Keep up the good work and for God's sake, let's get this system fully operational again. Whatever it takes, I'll support you!"

Even through the sound-attenuating glass of the booth, Joshua hears the cheers erupt from the operations floor as the operators stand up at their monitors and cheer. Audrey simply smiles up at Joshua Hunt and nods her thankfulness.

Chapter 24

George rolls the extension cord back on its plastic spool as he walks out of the house and toward the pickup. At the truck, he pulls the plug from the outlet on the dash and turns off the ignition. The silence, after so many hours of the truck's exhaust noise, is almost deafening. He throws the extension cord and short two-by-four into the bed of the truck. He realizes he is famished and wonders where he can get some breakfast or even if he can get some breakfast. He doesn't have long to contemplate his hunger before Emma Lou comes bursting out of the screen door onto the porch.

"The lights are out again!" She shouts.

"Oh my God!" He runs for the house. In the back bedroom he finds Henry with a beet-red face struggling to remain calm.

George moves quickly behind the respirator and follows the ribbed plastic air supply hose to where it enters the removable cover on the back of the machine. He pulls off the cover and pulls the hose from its connection. He puts it to his mouth and blows. He waits a few seconds and blows again, mimicking the rhythm he heard the machine make for so many hours. After thirty seconds, he sees Henry relax and his color return to normal.

"You had me going there for a few minutes," Henry says, expending a lung full of air.

"Sorry about that old man. I never should have trusted Contran. They try to screw us every chance they get don't they?"

"They know how to hit a guy when he's down. That's for sure."

George hands the end of the plastic air hose to Emma Lou. "Emma you blow into this just like I did. Not too much though. I'll go out and get the truck running and this respirator running again. Then we're taking Henry to the hospital . . . no more chances. I'll round up some of the neighbors to help."

Emma Lou nods and starts blowing gently into the plastic hose just as George instructed.

Chapter 25

Carlos, carrying Maria, and Johnny Capello, supporting Martin Walters, both reach Elmhurst Hospital's main entrance at the same time. Johnny holds the door for Carlos then helps Martin in behind him. Carlos shouts to a passing nurse, "Help me please. My wife will lose her baby."

The nurse looks harried and totally confused. "Take her to the emergency room."

"Where?" he asks.

She points across the lobby to a set of swinging doors. The lobby is totally crammed with people waiting for treatment. Maria buckles with the force of another contraction, too weak to cry out. Carlos, too tired to carry Maria a step further, sits heavily on the floor. Johnny leans Martin against the wall beside the door and rushes to where a teenage boy sits in a wheelchair. The boy has an obviously broken wrist.

Johnny shouts, "Up!"

"What?" The boy is stunned.

"Get up," Johnny shouts, pulling the wheelchair back.

The boy finally stands and Johnny rushes the chair to where Carlos sits on the floor with Maria.

"Here, let me help." Johnny reaches down and lifts Maria from Carlos' arms. She is almost unconscious, frozen in contraction. Johnny sets her in a semi-sitting position in the wheelchair and rolls her toward the emergency room doors.

"Bless you," Carlos says, stumbling to his feet and following.

Johnny pushes the right door to the emergency area open with his arm and shoves the wheelchair through. "We have a very pregnant woman here," he shouts.

"We have a lot of more serious problems than that," a young intern retorts.

"My wife's baby will die," Carlos adds.

"I'm sure you're overreacting. She'll be fine. Women have been having babies ever since the Garden of Eden."

Johnny concludes that the intern is an educated, smart-ass idiot.

"What's this?" An older woman doctor asks as she's passing.

"Just another pregnancy," the intern announces for everyone to hear.

"Just another pregnancy, hell," Johnny shouts, "this woman is losing her baby."

"So you're a doctor?" The woman retorts.

"No, I'm not a doctor but I'm not an idiot either, like that jerk," he says nodding toward the intern.

"Talk to me quick. I don't have a lot of time." The woman turns to Carlos.

"She's been stuck in an elevator and her doctor said she's too small to have the baby."

"Who's her doctor?"

"I . . . across town near where we live."

"What's his name?"

Carlos' mind is a blank. He shrugs. "She . . . "

"For God's sakes, her name then."

He shrugs again.

"How long?"

"How long?" Carlos repeats the question, totally confused.

"How long in labor?"

"I don't . . . yesterday, before the lights go out?"

"Good Lord, the baby has got to be in severe distress, if it's even viable."

"Via . . ." Carlos furrows his brow.

"Never mind. Here, let me take her." The doctor hands her clipboard to Johnny and pushes the wheelchair up the hallway. She shouts, "I need a Gurney right now, someone, anyone, get me a Gurney. We've got to get this mother open and now!"

Two nurses come running with a rolling high steel bed in tow. The two nurses and the woman doctor hoist Maria onto the Gurney. Johnny looks down at the clipboard and then hands it to the closest nurse. She tosses it on the Gurney between Maria's spread legs and the trio heads quickly up the hallway. Carlos trots along behind.

Johnny heads back into the waiting area. He had totally forgotten about Martin Walters. He's sure Martin has forgotten about him and has snarfed a few times to boot, or at least tried to.

When he gets back to the entrance, Johnny finds Martin sitting on the floor, holding his throbbing head in his hands. "Oh, my head hurts!" he repeats over and over, not remembering ever having said it even once.

Johnny goes to the desk where people are standing three-deep with clipboards, filling out forms. He calls to the woman behind the desk. "There's a man out here in bad shape. He's been beaten pretty badly."

"Just fill out an admittance form." The woman hands a clipboard over the heads of the people closest to the desk.

"I'm not related. I don't even know the guy."

"You know his name?"

"Yeah."

"That's more than we know. Just fill out his name and whatever you know about his condition."

Johnny walks back to the entrance and sits on the floor beside Martin. "Hey man now you're giving *me* a headache. I don't do paperwork . . . hell, I don't even do homework." Johnny lifts the string attached to the clipboard and follows it to the pen at the end. He fills out the form, putting Martin Walters' name on the line for patient and putting in his own name and address as *friend*, crossing out the words *next of kin*. Upon seeing the word *kin*, he remembers that he hasn't been home in almost fifteen hours. "I'll bet my mother is worried sick."

Martin parrots, "Sick, I'm really sick."

"Oh, shut up. I've heard it six million times." Johnny's tone is not harsh, it is tired, very tired. He feels that he has come a long way. He has. Johnny Capello is a very different person from the person he was two days earlier.

Chapter 26

The emergency room door slides open and two men carry in a third man who looks as though he has been gutted in a Japanese harikari ritual. The man being carried looks to be wearing dark red pants but the pants are really khaki. The man on the wounded man's right is short and squatty like Lou Costello and the man on his left looks like Bud Abbott.

"What happened to him?" asks a good-looking blond nurse just inside the door.

"He was shot on the subway."

"Where?"

"Somewhere between thirty-seventh and forty-sixth streets," the Abbott look-alike says.

"What are you a comedian? Where did the bullet hit him?"

Costello replies, "In the right side."

"Just above the hip," Abbott finishes the sentence.

"Bring him over here. Can you get him up on this Gurney?"

"Sure, we hauled him all the way across town." Abbott takes another turn trying to make points with the pretty nurse.

"What kind of gun?"

Costello jumps in so he won't lose points, "Hell, we don't know. It was pitch black." The two men lift the semiconscious man onto the Gurney.

"Someone shot him when they couldn't see him?" The nurse puts a blood pressure cuff on the wounded man's arm and begins pumping it.

Abbott's quick to respond, "You got it, Lady."

"How can you shoot someone you can't see?"

"You just aim in the direction of the foul mouth."

"You'll be great witnesses for the police. You don't have any idea of what the guy looks like."

"She," Costello corrects.

"So you did see her?"

"No. We heard her," Abbott says.

Costello adds, "Just before our pal here said something like *great a woman on PMS with a gun*."

"Oh, a justifiable shooting."

"Justifiable?"Abbott does not look pleased.

An orderly and a doctor step up to the Gurney and the doctor begins examining the man's wound.

"Purely justifiable." The nurse's manner is matter-of-fact. "Now we'll take care of him. You two go out the waiting room through there." She points at a doorway.

To the doctor she says, "He's very shocky. B. P. is sixty-six over fifty-eight.

Chapter 27

George and three of Henry's neighbors load Henry and his respirator into the bed of the pickup truck. It's a complex task to keep Henry hooked up as they move everything outside to the truck. The three men horse the machine, the extension cord, Henry, and his wheel chair from the back bedroom, through the hallway and kitchen, and out the front door. The men lay Henry down on a comforter in the bed of the truck and Emma sits beside him. The respirator's electric cord runs through the sliding back window in the truck's cab and to the outlet on the dash. The respirator keeps supplying Henry's air with a comforting kawak . . . kawak . . . kawak sound.

George drives slowly in a low gear toward the hospital, keeping the truck's engine's rpm above twenty-five hundred but below three-thousand so the voltage at the outlet on the dash will stay about one-hundred-ten. He's afraid if the voltage drops too much below one-ten, the electric motor in the respirator will slow down too much, overheat, and burn up.

George had warned the management at Contran that if someone didn't mandate capacity reserve margins the whole power system would be in jeopardy. He had hoped that a blackout would come and show the idiots he was right. Now he can't believe he had wished this blackout on Henry. Before this he didn't really grasp the consequences of a widespread power failure. Like everyone else he imagined the inconvenience it would cause but he didn't really think of electric power in terms of the life-and-death consequences.

It is still two miles to the Sister's of Mercy Hospital and the gas gage needle is pegged at empty. The borrowed pickup is the only vehicle moving on the highway and George has to keep turning off the pavement onto the shoulder and driving over curbs and grass to get around abandoned cars. He prays that the gas gage reads on the low side.

As the truck passes one small bungalow George sees a teenage boy mowing the lawn. Behind the car in the driveway rests a gallon gasoline can. George pulls the truck to a stop. He places the short board between the accelerator pedal and the front edge of the seat to keep the engine speed up. He climbs out the truck and approaches the kid.

"Can you shut that thing off a second?" He shouts.

The boy shuts down the lawn mower and looks quizzically at George.

"I'm almost out of gas and I have to get the man in the back of my truck to the hospital so he won't die. Can I have that gas?" George points at the gas can behind the car in the driveway.

"It's not mine. I'm just mowing the lawn. It belongs to the owner of the house."

"Well, I don't have time to talk to him, so I'll just take the gas." George walks quickly over the back of the car and picks up the gas can. The can feels almost full.

The front door of the house opens and a willow-stick of man comes out onto the porch. The screen door slams behind him. "Hey, what's going on out here? Why aren't you mowing?" he yells at the kid.

"This man wants your gas."

"You can't mow the backyard without it."

"I have a dying man in the back of the truck I've got to get to the hospital and I'm running out of gas. I need this to get him there," George says holding the can higher.

"You New Yorkers may be rioting and burning and looting your own city but you aren't going to loot and steal up here."

"I'm not a New Yorker. I own a home just six miles from here."

"The tags on your truck say you're from New York."

"I borrowed the truck."

"Just like you want to borrow my gas."

"That's right."

The man goes inside quickly and comes out with a shotgun that he had resting just inside the front door. He points the gun at George. "Now you put that gas can back where it was and get your New-York butt off my property."

The color drains from George's cheeks. He quickly sets the gas can back down on the driveway and backs away with his hands out to his sides, shoulder high.

Emma Lou shouts from the back of the truck. "What's wrong with you? My husband might die and you won't give us a gallon of gas?"

"You all get out of here!" The man shouts.

George backpedals all the way to his side of the truck and climbs in. He pulls the board off the accelerator pedal and puts the truck in gear. He pulls away slowly.

As the truck passes the next house, an old man comes running out to the street. He's carrying a gas can much like the one George almost got shot for.

"Here. Take this. I heard Sam next door threaten you. This is only about three-quarters full but it'll help. He's not a bad guy but this blackout has made him crazy. I think it's because he can't watch his Baywatch titties, or Girls Jumping on Trampoline reruns on the boob tube."

"Thanks," George says out the passenger's side window as he stops the truck.

"Just sit there, I'll do it," offers the man.

"I'd appreciate it. I can't shut the truck down or slow the engine because it's supplying the power for a respirator in the back."

The man pulls open the gas flap, removes the gas cap and sticks in the spout of the gas can. He looks and Emma Lou and Henry in the bed of the truck. "Maybe I can siphon some gas from my car there." He points to the Pontiac in the driveway.

George answers quickly, "It won't work. The car isn't old enough. They put blocks inside the gas filler necks of cars after the seventy-three fuel embargo to keep people from stealing gas by siphoning it out."

"Oh, I didn't know that." The man is obviously disappointed. He tips the can up as high as it will go above the truck's filler pipe. "There, it's all in. I hope it helps." The man replaces the gas cap and shuts the gas flap.

"It's probably just what we'll need to save Henry's life," George shouts as he puts the truck in gear and pulls off.

"God bless you!" Emma Lou shouts over the tailgate of the truck to the old man holding the empty little red gas can.

"I'll pray for your husband!" He shouts.

George shakes his head as he examines the truck's gas gage. The needle hasn't budged.

The last two miles to the Sisters of Mercy Hospital are the longest George has ever driven. George is sweating like a steel handler in a Jersey welding shop, on the hottest August day. At any moment he expects the truck's motor to sputter and die.

It's only when he sees the top floor of the hospital over the trees along the roadway that George relaxes. They have made it. It is at this moment of ultimate relief that George hears the dreaded sputter of the engine. It misses and then catches again. It runs smoothly for several seconds more then coughs once more and dies completely.

George stops the truck, mashes down on the emergency brake pedal, and climbs out. He rushes around to the back of the truck, as he has practiced so many times before in his head, over the last two miles. He springs to the truck's step bumper, vaults the truck's tailgate and rushes to the respirator. He pulls off the back panel and yanks the end of the ribbed plastic respirator tube from its connection. He blows gently into the tube. Henry hardly has a chance to miss a breath.

Between breaths, George speaks. "Emma, we've got to get Henry out of the truck and into his wheel chair. Then we can roll him the last hundred yards to the hospital."

"It sounds like a plan," Emma is confident in George's abilities. He has proved time and again that he can get the job done, whatever it is.

Flat on his back, Henry's eyes are wide with panic but he says not a word. He's trying his best not to be a problem. He will be clay in Emma's and George's hands.

George hands the respirator tube to Emma. "Your turn. I'll get the wheelchair ready and then get Henry. You just blow every five seconds or so, but gently, just like before."

Five minutes later, George stands behind Henry's wheelchair at the Sisters of Mercy admissions' desk. Emma Lou is at his side, gently blowing into the ribbed respiratory tube. The admission clerk is too busy to notice them.

"Excuse me, Ma'am, but we have a serious problem here." George's voice is deep and loud and it shocks the clerk to attention.

The clerk looks up and sees Henry's ashen face and a large man and short old woman behind his wheelchair. "Make it quick. I'm very busy here."

George is quick, quick and firm, quick, firm, and loud. "Henry Hasings here can't live without a respirator and we need to get him on one now."

The clerk notes that Emma Lou is acting as Henry's respirator. "That lady is doing what we can't. We don't have any available respirators. Everyone is in use, sorry."

"We have a respirator in a pickup truck down the street. Do you have a room we can set it up in?"

"We have four patients in every double room. I don't see how we can put your friend in a room."

"Do you have an electrical wall plug anywhere in the building we can use?"

"We have patients hooked up to all kinds of machines in hallways and in waiting rooms all over the hospital. I don't know if there is an available plug anywhere in the building but I suspect there may be. Just don't ask me where."

"How about if I can find one? Can I use it?"

"Feel free to use any outlet you can find so long as it isn't in an operating room or in some room that's off limits to the patients and public."

George turns to Emma. "Keep it up, you're doing great. I'll find an outlet somewhere and get and set up the respirator. Then I'll come back and get you and George. Okay?"

"Okay," Emma whispers between breaths. She smiles. "We'll be fine."

George nods and runs back toward the entrance.

Chapter 28

Abbott and Costello are sleeping soundly, lying out on the carpet in the main waiting room. The pretty woman doctor kicks gently at Abbott's foot several times. He doesn't budge so she kicks his foot three times harder. Abbott blinks several times and sits up. He looks up and the doctor, squinting against the fluorescent lights backlighting her.

"What?"

"Sorry. Your friend didn't make it. He was in very severe shock from loss of blood. We gave him five units. His heart stopped six times and the last time we couldn't get it going again."

"Oh shit." Abbott lays back, dropping the back of his head onto the carpet. "He was a great guy. . . nasty mouthed but a great guy. He could really tell a joke."

"Yes, well it's good to be great at the important stuff . . . otherwise one's life might be considered meaningless." She turns and leaves.

"Uh huh," Abbott responds, appreciating the doctor's having said something deep and meaningful about his dead dear drinking buddy.

Chapter 29

The room is crowded with recovering mothers. Four beds are crowded into a room intended for two. Maria is in a bed near the window. She has an intravenous feed in her left arm and Carlos is at her side, holding her right hand.

"He's a handsome hombre." He smiles down at his love.

"Yes. He's strong too. What should we name him?"

"I thought we had decided to call him Josè after my grandfather."

"I am thinking different now."

Carlos turns his head and looks sideways at Maria. "Dean, after the gringo who saved me?"

"Would you mind?"

"No. I have thought about it also. Muy mucho. I was going to ask you if it would be okay to name him Dean Josè Managua."

"It is a good name, Carlos . . . un nombre realmente bueno." Maria's eyes glisten.

"Yes, a strong and brave name." Carlos raises her hand to his mouth and kisses it. "Le amo más que usted puede conocer a Maria."

Chapter 30

Jim Stepe and Elaine Mercer are on the air, with the Channel 7 logo centered on the fake wall behind them.

"It's nice to have all of our viewing public back with us. I'm sure you all have missed us as much as we've missed you." Jim smiles warmly.

Elaine adds, "As you all know, the summer blackout of 2005 is over and we're almost back to normal. The final tally is fifty-seven lives lost, sixteen of those in New York City, and we've yet to get an estimate on the total damages. Some project the actual cost in the billions. That's three to four billion dollars in lost work, lost sales, and damaged and destroyed goods and businesses over a fifteen-state area."

The camera switches back to Jim. "Yes Elaine and it's not only small businesses that have taken a hit. Stock prices have plummeted and trading on the markets was suspended at noon today. The chairman of the Federal Reserve issued a statement today saying that the panic selling we've been seeing on the American, New York and Nasdaq stock exchanges is only a temporary overreaction to the blackout and that the stock prices will likely recover soon without an adjustment in the federal interest rate. That's good to know and I'm sure all our viewers are confident in the Fed's assessment."

The camera switches back to Elaine. "On another front, the insurance companies are petitioning Congress for the authority to sue the federal government for the damages they have suffered. The insurance underwriters claim that the federal government itself is to blame for going ahead with deregulation when it didn't know how it would assure the class of electric service we Americans have grown to expect and need in order to function as a nation. The majority leader said this morning that he expects the house will pass a bill in just a matter of weeks allowing the class action law suit and that the senate will approve it quickly."

"Yes, Elaine," Jim adds as the camera switches back to him, "The president has indicated that he will not veto such a measure. He said in an interview, on the White House steps just this afternoon, that it's time the federal government owns up to its mistakes. He said he will appoint a blue ribbon commission of non-industry electric power experts to come up with recommendations on how we can best assure the nation maintains adequate generating and transmission capacity in a deregulated market. He said there has been far too much talk about going back to a regulated power market and that such a move would be impossible. In his words, *A deregulated power market is the only way to ensure our economic future. We just need to make some fine adjustments to get it back on track.* Again, those were his words. As for myself, I'll always be a bit nervous from now on, whenever I hear talk of deregulating another industry. How about you, "Elaine?"

"I think we'll all be a bit more nervous in the future, Jim. What is that saying? Once bitten, twice shy?"

Chapter 31

Martin Walters is sitting up in bed when the nurse comes in with his supper tray.

"Well?" He quickly asks, as she sets the tray on his bed stand.

"His name is Johnny Capello. He lives in the Bronx." She takes a notepad from her pocket and hands it to Martin.

He studies it a moment. "At this address?"

"Yes, with his mother. I called information and got the telephone number . . . it's there at the bottom."

"Thanks. I owe this kid. I've been remembering a lot. It was coming really slow at first but now it's all coming back."

"That's good. The doctor says it usually works that way with a trauma and concussion like yours."

"The kid saved my life. He also helped get a pregnant woman admitted into the emergency room so she wouldn't lose her baby."

"A busy do-good teenager, huh?"

"He's one of those rare *can-do* individuals you run into every once in a while."

"Yeah the world, at least New York, has its fill of the other kind, like the ones who ransacked half of Manhattan when the lights were out."

"Well this one can make something of himself . . . that is if he tries."

"Trying doesn't always do it. My cousin Vinny could make something of himself but his family doesn't have the resources to help. He'll probably be still be delivering pizzas when he's forty."

"Well, Johnny won't be delivering pizzas unless that's all he wants to do. I intend to pay for his college education if decides to go that route."

"Whooh, a college education nowadays isn't cheap."

"No, not cheap at all, and I'll foot the bill for the best school he can get into."

"What do you do for a living, if you don't mind me asking?"

"Personally, not much anymore. I used to be a stock broker."

"And now?"

"Now? Now I own a brokerage house in Philadelphia."

"You must be losing a bundle in the stock market then."

"Are you kidding? I'm making a killing."

"How's that?"

"I am the broker. I make money on every sale. It doesn't matter if the investor sells at a profit or a loss; I always make a profit. And, believe me, today there was a lot of buying and selling going on."

Epilogue

In September 2005 the senior senator from California will introduce the National Electric Reliability Bill. The legislation will rocket through the energy committees in both houses and will be signed into law October 15, 2005.

The proposed law will create an independent Federal Electric Reliability Commission, which will oversee and ensure reliable electric service throughout the country. The law will give the newly created commission the power to require every electric generating company selling wholesale power maintain a reasonable percentage of its owned generating capacity in reserve; the reserve percentage to be established by the Commission each year. In addition, the law will grant the Commission the authority to audit all sales contracts and spot sales to ensure that no generating company has violated the established reserve requirements. The Commission will have the authority to levy severe fines against noncomplying generating companies.

Words from the Author

My son, growing up, had the habit of really messing himself up doing radical things on skateboards, bicycles, snowboards, motorcycles, etc. Whenever he was recovering from one of his self-inflicted injuries, and I would chide him for not being more responsible, he would say, "Anything that doesn't quite kill you only makes you stronger." He was right — over the years he has grown into one tough individual.

That's the future of our nation under electric power deregulation. We will become a much stronger people, at least those of us who survive. Deregulation will bring us together as a nation, much as did World War II. We will be stressed, we will be tested, we will be inconvenienced, and we will be forced to improvise in order to continue our daily routines. There will be a common enemy who will regularly confront and challenge us and we will all have to work together to combat it. The nationally uniting common enemy will be the rotating-local or wide-area blackout.

God bless electric power deregulation! It will get us Americans off our collective, pampered, complacent butts. In the end, those of us who survive will be stronger, wiser, and better prepared to deal with adversity.

Printed in the United States
6446